Dish It Up, Baby!

Dish It Up, Baby!

A Novel by Kristie Helms

Firebrand Books

Cover design by Jonathan Bruns
Cover photo by Andy Caulfield/Getty Images
Book design by Toolbox DC

Printed in the United States

10 9 8 7 6 5 4 3 2 1

An application to register this book for cataloging has been submitted to the Library of Congress.

Helms, Kristie
Dish It Up, Baby!
ISBN 1-56341-134-2

Author's Note

I never know what to say about the World Trade Center that hasn't already been said. The tragedy, the overwhelming grief, the politics of that Tuesday reverberate through our lives each day as I'm sure they will for decades to come.

A good portion of this book takes place in the World Trade Center. I debated whether or not to change the location, but writers are taught to "write what you know." And I knew what it was like to work in the World Trade Center.

I knew that little thrill that came from walking each morning into the tallest buildings I had ever seen. I knew what it meant to have grown up surrounded by tobacco fields and ranch homes and trailer parks and to dream wide enough and work hard enough that you could find yourself sitting in a conference room above one of the most powerful cities in the world. I knew what it was like to find your office building on postcards.

I often see bumper stickers now that read, "We Will Remember 9/11/01" and I know that I never want to forget what the towers were like before that day. Before they became something else. Because while it is important to remember that Tuesday, it is just as important to remember what the World Trade Center was like. Before.

September 8, 2003

Dedication

This book would not have been possible without the love, support and inspiration of my role model and sister Katie. She has been with me every step of the way. A super-special thanks to Becca, Jessie, Toni and Kevin for their friendship, passion and continuous stream of emails. And all my love to Kathryn. You are my treasure.

Preface

I MADE a habit of going for walks at lunch. It kept my 9-to-5 routine sane, and I had once learned from Lloyd, my first boss, that leaving the workplace for the entire lunch hour kept everyone honest. (I imagined Lloyd just wanted to make sure no one was sneaking into the petty cash while he was over at the Dairy Dip sucking down cheeseburgers and shakes.) And even though New York City was a long way from Lloyd back in Possum Trot, Kentucky, his advice still made sense to me.

It was on one of those lunchtime walks that I found myself standing in the middle of a crowd searching for soups or sandwiches or whatever lunchtime crowds searched for. I found myself standing in this pressing crowd in mid-March with the afternoon light bouncing off Rockefeller Center just at the entrance to the Sixth Avenue trains. I found myself holding on for dear life to a woman I had known through emails and letters and phone calls for years, and had only met in person the day before.

I drank in Laura and the smell of her blue wool coat.

I felt her lips brushing my cheek. Whispers in my ear. Pleads to leave my husband and move away from his fists. Phrases of running off and cats and long brunches and sunlight. My husband had moved me away from my family and friends in the South to New York City. He screamed at me whenever I left the apartment, and in the three years we had lived in Manhattan, I had managed to make friends only through online communities and emails. One of them had come to visit and after a day of roaming the city with her, I pressed my cheek into her blue wool coat trying to make her more real. Half-prayers raced through my mind.

Holy Mary Mother of God. Where are you? Where are the white train and the lilies of the valley and the four proper bridesmaids all in a

Nothing was the same in my marriage after Laura hugged me. I was no longer able to play the game that kept me from getting hit. I couldn't smooth the rough edges or calm my voice when talking to my husband's anger. His fist fell on my thighs more often in the days after that hug. It'd fall when I'd get the answer to his questions wrong. When I didn't wake up fast enough or go to sleep slowly enough. I forgot which I was supposed to do when. It all ran together.

I tell people now that I left him because it was a bad marriage. But I don't know that it was a real marriage to begin with. At the wedding rehearsal, my priest asked me, "What do you want? What do you want from this marriage? Why do you need to get married?" I didn't know how to answer. I hadn't washed my hair that day and I felt greasy. My new contacts were burning my eyes and I couldn't think properly. I just stared at him. Father looked at me and said, "You want to be happy. You just want to be happy."

It wasn't until Laura whispered to me that I understood, finally, what he meant. What it was to be happy. I wanted Laura to come back to New York City. I wanted my own apartment, where she could whisper to me again, and I decided to leave my marriage.

I left my husband from the safety of my cubicle located on Sixth Avenue in the heart of midtown Manhattan. It was a tall, black steel building with security guards, and it was the place where his shouting and slapping couldn't get to me. The hours between 9 and 5 were precious and I used every one of them in the 30 days between Laura's whispers and the moving van. I sat in my cubicle and compiled budgets and checklists. I reserved movers, set up my own bank account and pored through apartment listings. I divided our assets and debts.

I started pricing various items around the apartment based on the value of my pain. A racist comment on the train equaled four feather pillows. Waking to a bruise on my shoulder was the equivalent of a VCR. I talked to my therapist a lot. She asked me an incredibly long list of questions and ended one of our sessions with my name, address and cross streets written neatly in her personal book. She handed me her emergency beeper number after I mentioned a bloody nose. I told her I believed it had been caused by my husband's fist in my face. She said, "If 911 comes across this beeper I'll know it's you and I'll call the police."

It was all logistics during the 9-to-5. I came up with the security deposit for another apartment and wrote out a script to tell my parents, who lived a two-hour plane ride away in Nashville. The planning was easy. The hardest part was being *so close* to freedom.

People always want to know why women stay in abusive relationships. Why they don't leave the first time they're hit. It all seems so simple doesn't it? Hit. Leave. Hit. Leave. The math is simple. Two plus two equals out the door. But it wasn't easy. And what I want to tell people, but never do, is that it can happen to anyone because it happened to me. We were the couple who didn't fit any of the stereotypes. We had college degrees, no alcohol and no drugs. I would sometimes stare at domestic violence posters trying to fit myself into their vision of a greasy-haired woman crouching in a corner and it wasn't me. I had good suits and a nice haircut. I told myself that he didn't hit that hard and that I had crouched in a corner only once. Or twice.

He didn't hit that hard and he loved me. And after a few years of being told that I was fat and lazy and stupid and a whore and ugly and unsuccessful. And a bitch. And a bitch. And a bitch. Somewhere in there, the world became so bizarre and unexpected if I didn't anticipate just right. I mean if I didn't guess what breakfast he was going to want on Sunday morning. If I failed to say the right thing when a bus. A city bus, mind you. When a city bus failed to materialize according to schedule. If I. God. If I crossed the street from a direction different than the one he expected. The curses would begin and the fists would reach out. My world would spin rapidly out of control.

My shoulder would be jerked back as I tried to sink into the bed and hide. Tried to dig down under the covers. Become one with the mattress. Slide into the coils. And I'd be jerked around at one a.m. to answer for my sins. He would scream that I had somehow allowed the computer to malfunction and then refused to take it in to be fixed. He screamed that I had thrown out something he needed for work. I had been cleaning as I thought good housewives did and I threw it out and his fist came down on my thigh. A hand. Big. And harsh. And thick. Crashed into my face. And there was. Blood. And he screamed. He yelled "bitch, stupid loser" until I forgot which word meant what. And I whispered to myself,

No more.

The more steps I took toward leaving, the easier it got. I started to picture what it would be like for him to come home from his trip to Seattle and find me gone. An empty apartment spread out before him. I wanted to watch him navigate the grocery aisles for the first time. I wanted to laugh as he figured out how to do his laundry. I'd picture the rage on his face. And it sent my heart to a place behind walls where even I thought I could forget about it.

I called and made an appointment to see an apartment. It was in Brooklyn and a good 40-minute subway ride away from him in Manhattan. It was perfect. A basement apartment in the house of a rabbi and his family. It was three entire rooms, with no broker's fee required. The security and deposit were negotiable. The landlords, who were busy getting ready for Passover, asked me a couple of questions. They saw the pain on my face. The wife turned to me and said,

"You're like our daughter. We want you to be happy. You give us a small check and the apartment is yours."

I realized then that he had been wrong. For years, he told me that I was unsuccessful. A financial drain. But I had run the numbers and the budgets and the analysis and I knew for a fact that I could do it without him. I realized that I was not the bitch. I was not a loser. I was not his version of me.

I was, however, still a good Catholic girl and before I left for good, I tried to talk to him. Tried to figure something out. A last-ditch effort that began with him talking so sweetly. I would get suckered in. Sucker. It ended in a screaming match when I refused to back down like I usually did.

The thing was. The thing that I usually didn't tell anyone. Was that I did love him. I did. I wanted to be married to him. But I couldn't live there. I couldn't make those two thoughts make sense. I didn't know if it mattered whether or not it made sense and I didn't know if I cared.

The week before the move, I could no longer eat. I drank protein drinks to keep from fainting. I had lost 20 pounds in two weeks and could only stare blankly at the freckled girl on the side of the Fresh Samantha bottles that kept me alive. In kindergarten we had these mimeographed sheets with smiling faces, sad faces and angry faces. It was our duty to label each one correctly. Identify the emotion. I wanted that sheet back. I wanted one already labeled neatly with a nice red check at the top indicating I'd completed the exercise correctly.

I felt unchecked. Incorrect. I labeled myself sad to be leaving. That I wouldn't get to hug him any more or hear the little jokes that he made. I wouldn't get to rub his head. Or watch him try to make friends with the cat. I was sad that on Tuesday morning he would leave the apartment happy. And I would never see him happy again. I would never get to kiss him or hold him or laugh with him again.

I labeled myself angry that I had to leave at all. That he couldn't take one step. Couldn't go to one lousy counseling session. Wouldn't listen to one of my issues. Thought it was "OK" to get so angry that his fists flew. Thought it was "OK" to make up for that by saying, "Sorry."

I labeled myself frustrated that I had spent so much time on my marriage. That I didn't listen to my heart or the universe when I had a chance. I kept thinking things *would* be okay — somehow. I had believed him when he cried. I thought he knew what he was saying when he whispered, "I'm sorry, and I'll never, ever do that again." I thought that I was unlovable, unwanted, unnecessary. I didn't know how to live life without getting married, so I did. And I figured I'd be able to fix his anger later. When later came, his curses and yelling convinced me that I had been wrong. Defective. He told me I was stupid and fat and ugly and a bitch. And I came to believe it.

I labeled myself excited to be allowed a new chance. To be strong enough emotionally and financially to see what else was out there. To be able to have my own space.

I labeled myself scared that I wouldn't be able to make it. That I'd end up having to move to my parent's house. Or that I'd step down into the subway one evening after work and he'd be there with that rage in his face.

One month after the hug, three weeks after locating the new apartment and four days after the fist and the blood, he went on a business trip to Seattle, and I moved out of the marriage and into Brooklyn.

Everything else happened after.

 chapter

1

WHEN the movers left me in Brooklyn with half my marriage packed in cardboard around me, there were open spaces in my mind for the first time since I had signed that marriage license. It was hard to get used to. All that time free from not having to pack a lunch for him to take to work. Free space from not having to plot to keep the peace. To keep a meat and three plus dessert on the table nightly. To keep the floors scrubbed. All that space and I was rattling around in it.

I spent a lot of my newly-freed time polishing my grandmother's silver. I set out a lace tablecloth. I put fresh flowers in the kitchen window and took long bubble baths with lotions and soaps and tea-lights and Patsy Cline on the stereo. Sometimes it helped.

When I called my friends and family to tell them I had moved out I told them only, "It had been bad." No one asked any details. I didn't volunteer any. They all called me strong and brave, but I didn't feel strong or brave. I wondered. I wondered why no one had told me what they were telling me now. That they knew he had been bad. He had been wrong. They had seen the holes in the walls, heard the names he called me. Saw him yank on my arm, punch my thighs, yell. They had all heard him yell. And they had all stepped away. Walked out of the room. Pretended they didn't see. What was between a husband and a wife stayed between a husband and a wife. I wanted to blame them. Make it their fault for not having told me their fears. Validate my bruises. I wanted to blame anyone but myself for having stayed with him. In the days after I left, I never once blamed him.

I had a large, looming, empty feeling in the pit of my stomach that I tried to fill with chocolate-covered peanuts, Budweiser and Spaghetti-o's. For the first time in my life, I was completely on my own. I felt too small for the world. For the first four weeks, I closed off half of the apartment and lived only in the living room. I confined my feelings to the couch and the bathroom. At first, I unfolded the sofa bed to sleep at night, making myself comfortable by smoothing out quilts and sheets and tucking in the corners. It grew to be too much trouble, so I just lay down on top of the couch and pulled the sheets up over myself.

I realized the empty feeling had less to do with missing him and more to do with thinking that I had wasted my life. I had gotten married at 21 and I had missed out.

I listened to my friends' conversations and realized that people my age were talking about easing up on their drinking. I had never started. People my age talked about books they had read and plays they had seen while I was busy making sandwiches for him. People my age talked about concerts they had seen while I was, what? Trying to tune in any goddamn country music station I could find in a goddamn apartment the size of a box in a goddamn city that I only fucking moved to because he screamed and said we had to.

I needed to make up for lost time. I plotted one night to get myself drunk on a bottle of white wine I picked up near my subway station. I walked the mile home with my bottle and realized I didn't have a corkscrew. I didn't know I needed a corkscrew to open a bottle of wine. I was 27 years old and didn't know how to open a bottle of wine. My family was a mix of working class Southern Baptists and

Catholics and none of that made them wine drinkers. If you drank anything, it was a pull-top Budweiser that you kept more hidden than you thought you should have to. My college days had been spent at a school located in a dry county. I understood that the fraternities and sororities had keg parties, but I had started dating him in college and he refused to allow me to join a sorority. I prided myself on being the good girl then and had "gone South" over the state line to drink only on special occasions.

We never drank when we were married. We kept to our own apartment. There wasn't enough money to do anything more than go to the movies. The nightlife swirling around us seemed too much somehow. We would come home after work and not go back out again until the alarm clocks went off. Before I moved out of my marriage, I had been inside a bar only a handful of times. And I had never ordered a glass of wine.

I wanted something familiar. Something easy. I kept whispering to myself, "I want to go home," but I wasn't sure any more where home was. I was surrounded by cardboard boxes in my new apartment in a neighborhood of Orthodox Jewish families. Their fundamentalism only made me homesick for the Southern Baptists of my youth. I craved sweaty glasses of iced tea, wide-open spaces, sundresses and Sunday socials. Potluck dinners with potato casseroles done a hundred different ways. Grandmother cheating and putting Kentucky Fried Chicken extra crispy blend in one of her own bowls. I craved a cast iron skillet filled with Mamma's cornbread. And white beans. And laughter. And Uncle Earl's stories about the hardware store. And my girl cousins' tales of their latest romances. And my boy cousins riding up to the porch on their three-wheelers.

I needed to be rooted. To be grounded. To know where I was. I didn't know what to hold onto.

I wanted to get settled in the new apartment. Make it feel mine. So I threw away all my towels. My towels, for the most part, had been given by well-meaning relatives at wedding showers. They had been selected in the appropriate colors and wrapped, and when I received them, I had smiled and said, "Oh yes, how lovely. Thank you." Later the women had all clustered around the coleslaw and potato salad and fried chicken and I had continued to say all the right things.

"He's so caring, so sexy. Oh he is, isn't he?"

But it wasn't. It wasn't caring and it wasn't sexy. And God help me, it wasn't anything I was interested in unless I heard that catch in his voice. The one that meant I was treading on thin ice and only then did I become very interested.

He would never kiss me. He hated kissing and I craved it so much. He would say things. They were never caresses of words. Never, "I love you." Or those sweet nothings that movies always went on about. I would try to force those words out of his mouth. Tried to force the kisses. Tried so hard. Instead, it was the same thing every time. Years of him saying, "Let's do it." And me following him into the bedroom. He would lie on the bed and not move. Not once except to grip or pull my hair or hold my head. After I had made the appropriate motions and sounds learned from watching the porno movies he incorporated into those little sessions, there were no sweet kisses. No gentle words. He'd stand up. And walk. Into the bathroom. And pick up one of those goddamn towels.

The new towels didn't quite fix everything. I cried and while the tears didn't flow as much as I could have let them, the balance had shifted from being scared to being sad. I was beginning to realize that he had cared. He had loved me. He had loved me enough to worry if I was late getting home at night. He had been the one person who knew where I was at all times. He had cared and I had just left him without even saying good-bye. I had packed the good china and the porcelain bride and groom that had stood on top of our cake. I left my wedding dress in a bag under the bed and a pile of dirt where our couch had been. I wrote a two-page note detailing both the assets and the debts I was taking with me. I had not left a forwarding address. I had kissed him on the lips as he walked out the door to his business trip, knowing that I would never see him again.

I didn't know what kind of person would do something like that.

I couldn't convince myself that I had done the right thing by leaving.

 chapter
2

PEOPLE always wanted to know, "What do you miss? What do you miss about him?" I could never think of an answer. An answer that would adequately explain the tears I kept crying.

I missed coming home to him. Missed his smell. I missed matching place settings and casserole pots with proper lids and meals that were on time and our series of well-ordered weekends. Meats and threes and drives to see his parents. I missed the old Christmas cards that I'd saved and the other boxes of things I had left under the bed in my haste to leave.

There are hard decisions to make when you move out of a marriage. Especially when you're trying to do it without the other person knowing. I knew the goldfish I had been nurturing along wouldn't be able to make the move, so I put him to sleep by putting him in the freezer. I figured going to sleep in cold water was better than flushing him into the city's sewer system and all of that was better than him flipping out of the tank and landing on the Brooklyn Queens Expressway at rush hour.

My cat Maggie, though, was another matter. Maggie was my one true love. My best friend.

My Maggie had come into my life on a particularly bitter cold day in 1998 when I picked her out of all the others at the Manhattan ASPCA. She was eight years old and needed someone to love. I could relate. I spent two hours deciding which cat to bring into my life. It was not love at first sight. She didn't leap into my arms and I didn't leap into hers. We came together on one another's terms. She was the only cat there who would let me pet her and play with her. I carried her home. We fell in love after a brief courtship. He had tried to make friends with Maggie. He didn't want her, but he loved animals. That was the thing about him. I had to admit he had a heart, even when it was easier to pretend that he didn't. He told me Maggie was my responsibility. I thought he might take to her and figure out how to love.

When Maggie first came into the apartment, she climbed up on top of his computer. He screamed at her. I constructed a cover out of cardboard that I would slip over the monitor every night to keep him from yelling at Maggie again. He insisted we get an automatic litter pan that swept away Maggie's clumps so he wouldn't smell her. Maggie wasn't a foot high and even she took up too much room in the apartment.

When my marriage was crumbling around me, Maggie would lick my tears. And when he directed his rage at me, Maggie would position herself between us. When he raised his voice, Maggie took refuge under the desk. I wanted to join her.

After I moved to Brooklyn, Maggie and I grew closer. We had more time for one another. She reveled in the new space. She talked to me more often. She jumped from window sill to window sill fascinated by the squirrels that came right up to the windows of the basement apartment. When friends phoned, Maggie would curl in my lap contented. She would wait by the door when she knew it was time for me to come home, perched in her little meatloaf position, in a spot where she could see the entire apartment. When I walked in the door, she would leap up and come over for kisses. When I was late, she would berate me for making her worry.

Every evening when I came home, Maggie followed me into the bedroom to give me a hug. As I sat on the bed to undress, Maggie stretched out with her weight on her back feet, put a paw on each of my shoulders and rubbed her head under my chin. I'd kiss her over and over with loud smacks. She could anticipate my next move and race to wherever I was headed. When I was doing bills, she'd jump up onto the table and sit on whichever statement needed paying. When I was sobbing in the tub, she'd stick her paws over the side and peer in at me with a worried look. While I got ready in the morning, Maggie would sit on my feet in front of the bathroom sink. When I used the toilet, she'd use her litter box. We were in sync.

Maggie never tried to steal anything off my plate until I tried to eat latkes. That was the first sign My Maggie was Jewish. Later, she took to knocking the crucifix off the wall, turned her nose up at shellfish and refused to move on Saturdays. Maggie was also a male, though the ASPCA had put an "F" for female on all of her forms. I figured if she was queen enough to fool them, then who was I to say? So Maggie she remained, referred to by everyone from my mother to the vet as a "she" at both her and my insistence. Friends told me I was the only person they knew with a Jewish transgender cat.

Two months and two weeks after I moved to Brooklyn, Maggie got sick. I put her in her carrier and walked her two miles to the nearest vet. He kept her overnight and I found a credit card that could carry the $1,000 bill. When I brought her home the next day, she stumbled a lot. The anesthesia wasn't wearing off well and the vet sounded worried. He asked me to bring her in after the weekend. That night, Maggie went to sleep curled up on my pillow with her forehead on mine. She had never done that before. She was sicker than I thought.

That Monday the vet laid the options out for me. It would be another $2,000 to give Maggie the surgery she needed. They couldn't guarantee anything. They said, with her condition, that the surgery probably wouldn't help. My credit cards had been maxed out by the move to Brooklyn. I didn't have anything left. She was sicker than I could afford to fix.

I stroked her chin as she went to sleep for the last time in the back room of that cheap vet's office. She purred and I sobbed. I walked back to the apartment carrying her empty cat carrier. I stopped at every street corner and sat down to cry. The tears hurt my chest. A carload of young boys drove by and yelled at me. When I got back to the apartment, I was confronted with Maggie's toys. Her cat-nip balls, her litter box, her food bowls. I lay down on the floor in front of the door and I couldn't move. It was too much. I didn't know how much more the world could extract from me. Piece by piece there was nothing left. I had lost my last name, my home, my family, and my money. When that was gone they took Maggie. Two days later, I received a sympathy card from my vet and a bill for the $200 required to put her to sleep.

I paid it and called Laura. Again. I had called her almost every night since I left my marriage. Every night for almost three months, I called her long-distance. It seemed a lifetime ago that she had whispered to me in front of that subway station, and I tried to relive through telephone calls that touch of her hand, the pull of her arms on my shoulders, the feel of her eyes looking into mine. It had been the first rush of feeling I had ever had and I longed for it again.

I would talk about all the things I wanted to see, all I wanted to do, until I heard Laura's voice growing sleepy and her wit soften. Her voice would drop and she would tell me things. She would tell me that Maggie had loved me well and I had been right to bring her to Brooklyn. She told me that Maggie had loved watching the squirrels from her new windows and enjoyed having me all to herself without having to hide from him.

She would whisper, "Sweet dreams." And she would say, "I love you." And I would close my eyes and whisper, "I love you, too."

There wasn't a day that passed that I didn't think about Laura. I found myself touching my own cheek in the place that Laura had touched it. I walked past the spots in Manhattan where we had hugged. I detoured through Grand Central Terminal so I could remember the smile in Laura's eyes as I looked up at the stars.

On all those walks, I wondered if I were hopelessly heterosexual. I had never given any thought to being gay until Laura hugged me. She was the first lesbian I had ever met and after she hugged me, she was all I could think about. That snap of emotion felt like getting my first pair of glasses, in the fourth grade. We had driven back from the optometrist and I stared out the car window with my face glued to the glass. The world seemed sharper and I turned to my mother and said, "I never knew that you were supposed to be able to see the leaves on the trees."

Laura's blue wool coat struck me with the same clarity as the leaves on the trees along U.S. Highway 62.

I wondered if a person's sexuality could be based on having been with only one man. I wondered if my feelings for Laura were some kind of experiment. I thought maybe I was a battered woman looking for a softer experience or perhaps a 27-year-old wanting to explore. I ran through the possibilities, asked myself a litany of questions, contemplated old schoolgirl crushes and rushed home to call Laura every night.

I hung on her every word. Carefully planned speeches flew out of my head. Thoughtfully designed conversations took leave and I held onto her words. She read me poetry, whispered her great plans and listened to mine. She was a history professor at a small Minnesota college, had lived in England, visited Poland and done research in Germany. She had a passport, hundreds of books and the ability to live in any country that caught her fancy. I wanted to feel that free. That intelligent. That world-weary. We talked about going to Prague. I bought guidebooks and maps of the Czech Republic. I wanted to know as much about the country as she did. I didn't want to look stupid next to her. I wanted to know Prague through long walks down its city streets, not tracing lines in a guidebook.

Laura had had given me the confidence to leave my marriage. She had come to New York for a conference and I offered to show her around Manhattan. I had gotten to know her "virtual self" and the fact that she was gay through an online community in which we both participated. It was one of those places on the Web where people posted about their day, about their politics and even about the books they were reading. Most people used the place as an escape from the tedium of work. I used it as an escape from my husband. Online was the one place I could be away from him. It was where I could be me.

During Laura's visit, I showed her the Museum of Modern Art, Lincoln Center and Central Park. She fell in love with the city and I fell in love with her. I had spent so many years in my marriage saying nothing, and I found myself telling her everything. I told her about my marriage and about the yelling. I told her about the bruises and the blood and how much I loved the Brooklyn Bridge.

The day after our tour around the city, she called me at work to ask if we could meet on my lunch hour. I wanted to impress her. To make her like me as much as she liked the city. I held her hand as I led her through Grand Central Terminal, past the murals in the lobby of the Chrysler Building and through the Reading Room of the New York Public Library. She wrapped her arm around my waist as the hour came to a close and I walked her back to the subway so she could make her way to the airport. Strands of her long, blonde hair blew across my face as she held me close and whispered in my ear. She told me that women didn't have to live with men who hit them. She told me that I didn't need him to make it. That I could do it without anyone's help. She pushed my hair behind my ears and told me I was worth it. Worth being loved, worth feeling happy again, worth someone caring about me.

I believed her.

After I left the marriage, I called Laura nightly so she would tell me more. I wanted to be reminded of why I had left. To have someone tell me it would get better. That the pain would stop, that it would get easier to live on my own, that I didn't need a wedding ring to prove I was someone worth loving.

chapter

3

AFTER all my wishing and phone calls to her in Minnesota, Laura came to visit. She stayed with me in my new Brooklyn apartment — the one I had secured in the hope that she would come back to New York. In the hope that I could recapture that initial rush of feeling I first discovered with my cheek pressed up against her blue wool coat. It had been four months since she had hugged me and my entire world had changed. Laura had changed too. With all the phone calls, she was becoming more real. Less fantasy.

We sat in my new Brooklyn apartment and listened to Marianne Faithfull CDs. We drank vodka and ate latkes. We rode city buses and saw an African-American cowboy setting a Hasidic child on the back of a pony. We walked all over Brighton Beach, saw *Cabaret* on Broadway, ate seafood in the East Village and were mistaken for a couple by the waiter. We walked through Central Park and spent hours and hours in the Jewish Museum, at the fountain at Lincoln Center, around Brooklyn's Park Slope and walking Prospect Park. We toured the Bronx Zoo and ate roast duck in Chinatown.

We lay together in my darkened bedroom, where white Christmas lights flashed over a 1962 concert poster of Patsy Cline, and I touched my knee to the back of her thigh as we both pretended to sleep. We both pretended that the conversation we had during her first visit – the one that had landed us here – had never happened. Laura had set a chain of events into motion by telling me I could be loved, and while she still believed in the theory, she had no desire to be the person responsible for its day-to-day execution.

We had been drinking. Laura had, in fact, been drunk when she turned to me and said, "I feel like I should jump your bones and just get this whole coming-out thing over with for you."

I held up the Stoli bottle and said, "If it's a should and not a want, then you can just keep away from me."

And that was all. That was it. That was everything that was ever said between us. I had told her to keep away from me, but I couldn't keep away from her. I went to sleep that night holding a strand of Laura's hair. I told myself that I had to stop needing so much. I had to stop feeling. I had to stop putting the weight of this emotion on everyone around me because it would make them go away.

She flew back to Minnesota. I spent the next few weeks pushing her and her hug to the back of my mind. Our nightly phone calls became weekly conversations. And when even those became too strained, she stopped calling altogether.

The dreams, the vodka, the cleaning, the days and nights I spent sleeping the hours away. I'd been gone four months and still could allow myself to feel the pain only once a night, when I sat in my pink bathtub and cried. I wanted to get to the bottom of those tears as quickly as I could. I wanted to know how far down the hurt went and why it was still there. I told myself I never loved him and that he didn't love me. Neither of those phrases helped, because I couldn't make either of them true.

As long as I had been married and had that ring on my finger, I was able to tell myself that I was cared for. Even with the screaming, I could tell myself that a marriage license meant that I was loved. I ignored the madness and reminded myself that the Catholic Church told me I was worthy since I had a husband.

And then. I wasn't. And then. I was alone.

There were nights in the months after I left that I would wake up in a cold sweat remembering the last days I had spent with him. They weren't scenes of blood and bruises and nights spent waving kitchen knives to keep him away. What woke me up in a cold sweat were memories of those last weeks spent with him, when I had full knowledge of exactly who he was.

Even after I had figured out that I needed to leave. Even after I had tasted that rush of pure feeling on Laura's blue wool coat. Even then, I still had to lie there nightly, next to him, and go through the motions. Go through the motions of being a wife, on the pain of letting up the charade. On the pain of his discovering that I was making plans to leave. Nightly for a month before I could leave. Nightly still being a wife. Being a Wife. Nightly. For a month.

I wasn't sure if I was lesbian, bisexual, or just confused. I checked out every video on "the lesbian experience" available through the New York Public Library. I wandered around feminist bookstores studying the girls with their arms wrapped around other girls. I attempted to justify my feelings through independent validations and all I knew is that I wanted. Simply. To recapture that pure longing I had felt with Laura lying next to me. I had never wanted anyone the way I had wanted her. Ached to run my toe down the length of her leg while she lay wrapped in my grandmother's quilt on my bed in Brooklyn.

I had found a subtle crack between my past need to walk down the aisle and my current ache to place my hand on the curve of a woman's waist. I needed to know more. I made it my mission to seek out a real love and to live without casseroles for dinner and rings on my finger.

I pored over the personal ads. I filled my day planner with first meetings of the women I met through those ads. And none of them ever seemed to go anywhere. I wanted love so badly. I wanted to prove to myself that I could be the lesbian I thought Laura's blue wool coat had made me. There was Diana from San Francisco and Kelly from Staten Island. There was a girl my sister's age I took to a bluegrass concert. I had no idea how take anything further and I wasn't entirely sure that I wanted to.

One Sunday afternoon I had coffee in the West Village with a woman named Nancy. She looked just like a childhood friend. On that resemblance alone, I found myself actually being honest with her. Telling her about this "coming-out process" as I had begun calling it. Telling her about the marriage and the things I thought about doing with Laura. And Nancy talked back, with her curly black hair and her huge, brown eyes.

But dating wasn't enough. The phone calls weren't filling me up and I wasn't finding a way to get to the bottom of my tears. My birthday was coming up so I started planning. I wanted to go all out. I had always looked forward to my birthdays and they had fallen a little short the years I was married. That's how I put it. That "my birthdays fell a little short." They actually fell a lot short. It was my 22nd birthday, the first one after I was married, that set the standard for the rest of them.

I don't remember what started the fight. I have no idea. I just remember lots of screaming. I suggested to him that we take a drive. It's harder to hit when you're driving. (That's just a little FYI from the battered woman's handbook.) Plus, a change of scenery sometimes calmed him down. So on my birthday eve, the first year that we were married, we drove to the city park and we sat in the hot car and continued the screaming. He kept punching my arm. Over and over and over. God. I don't even remember what it was about. I think I asked him what he got me for a present. He always said I made too big a deal out of birthdays and he refused to get me anything because of that. He punished me. Punished me for enjoying birthdays.

I went into work the next day. It was August and it was insanely hot. I had to wear long sleeves to cover the bruises. To make matters worse, my mom sent me a huge bunch of balloons for my birthday. I tried to carry them to the car. I couldn't open the door because I couldn't lift my arm and hold the balloons at the same time. I started crying. I didn't know what to do. I had to take those balloons home.

That was my 22nd birthday. I have no idea what happened on my 23rd and 24th. On my 25th, I stole his credit card and bought myself a ticket to my parents' house in Nashville. My 26th we did absolutely nothing. There was no card. No present. Nothing. I was told that if hadn't made such a big deal out of my birthday I might have gotten something. But I had screwed things up by looking forward to my birthday. On my 27th, we went out to eat pizza and he complained — the whole time — about how much he hated his job and how bad our server was. But my 28th, I was on my own for the first time. It was my 28th birthday when it all changed. Because my birthday that year. Kicked ass.

I planned everything myself. There were 12 friends and Nancy, gathered around the table at the Cowgirl Hall of Fame restaurant in Manhattan. I thought it seemed an appropriate venue for a girl who had her very own stuffed rooster. "Hank" had been my birthday present to myself. I had bought him a few days earlier from a guy selling such things from the back of his station wagon near my subway stop.

For this birthday party, no one screamed and people brought me poetry. Poems they loved, books of poetry, poems they made up on the way to the restaurant. After we ate, we walked Nancy's dog around the West Village. One of my friends stopped on a side street and did a Mexican step dance she learned while working at Disneyland. We found a quiet bar where we downed a few more beers and then a smaller group of us made our way back to my apartment.

chapter

4

LIFE started to feel luscious again. I cried less. I no longer drank alone. I had more energy. I read a lot of poetry. I strung up more white Christmas lights and I walked into my bathroom and realized that I had the power to decorate it solely in pictures of Laura Petrie without anyone to belittle me for it. So I did.

I thought a lot about the first night I had spent in New York City. My husband and I had flown into Newark and by the time we made our way into Manhattan, I was completely overwhelmed. The city seemed too fast, too loud, too much and I wanted to go home. That wasn't an option, so we walked the avenues and cross streets searching for something to eat. I had no idea where to go and I was exhausted. I just wanted to stop walking. We stumbled into a diner. I had never been in a diner. The menu was six pages long.

I started crying.

Our waitress came over, took one look at me and my tears and told me that I needed to order the salmon. She wouldn't let me have the Coke I tried to ask for, and instead brought me a large glass of milk, "for your bones." I told her I was new in town and I didn't know what to do. That I had never been in a city this big and now I was supposed to live in it. I told her I needed a job, an apartment and

I didn't think I could do it. I told her I was scared that people would take advantage of me and afraid I'd fall apart from the strain of trying to hold everything together.

She told me I needed the green peas.

When we finished eating, she brought the check over and sat down at the table. She told us that the subways go "uptown" and "downtown" and that there are detailed transit maps posted in every station. She said I should hold my purse tight, but not too tight or people would think I was a tourist. She told me that her manager could help us find an apartment and she had written her home number down on the check for us. She told me that New York City was an incredible place to live and that every day I would find a power and strength on the streets that I had never felt before. She told me that living there was going to be a pain in the ass, but whenever I felt the city getting under my skin. Whenever it felt too difficult to go on. She told me that I should stand on the nearest street corner with my arms outstretched and my head held high and yell as loudly as I could,

"Go ahead and dish it up, baby!"

I went to Montreal to meet a group of people I knew from the Internet. I rode up through Boston and Vermont with one of them and made her my best friend. Rachel lived in Tucson but was planning to move back East as soon as she could. Rachel and I had been talking in an online community for over three years. She had been one of the people I would call on the pay phone whenever I could escape the apartment and my husband's yelling. When I'd call, she would tell me jokes and remind me that I knew how to laugh.

With the trip, I was testing out the waters. Flexing my skills at forming new relationships of all kinds. The rest of the summer I dated as much as I dared and went out as much as I could. I heard *Magnetic Fields* at the Knitting Factory and met the lead singer backstage. Nancy knew him and introduced us. Nancy also knew the music editor at *Time Out New York* and a singer named Lois whose cat-eye glasses I coveted. The opening act that night had been someone who played toy pianos. I tried to pretend I was a New Yorker and that toy piano player acts happened to me all the time. Instead, I felt very Possum Trot. Nancy and I were both trying to figure out if we were really lesbians. We made out on her couch but never seemed to move it any further.

I had gone on three dates with Nancy before the demons reared up on the one night I stayed in her apartment. I heard my husband's voice screaming at me. I had a nightmare that he was standing at the end of the subway steps. He wanted to grab me and carry me back into that world. I tried to cling to my world as tightly as I could. The world I was creating. But the nightmare caused me to tell Nancy I just wanted to be friends. I stopped having bad dreams and his yelling stopped ringing in my ears.

I spread poetry books around my apartment. I had found a copy of *This Is New York* by E.B. White on Nancy's bookshelf and I couldn't stop reading the rhythms of the city. I read poetry everywhere. I had never read poetry before and I couldn't get enough of it.

I carried Pablo Neruda's *100 Love Sonnets* with me. The version I had listed the English translation on the right side of the page and the Spanish on the left. One morning on the subway, as I was reading the English, the guy sitting to my left read the Spanish. He would signal to me when it was OK to turn the page. The subway seemed an ideal place for poetry. The Metropolitan Transit Authority had put up "Poetry in Motion" posters along the tops of the subway cars. Each of them featured a short snippet of a poem. I became obsessed with one called "Peaches" by Peter Davison. I didn't have a piece of paper to write it down, so I searched for it online. Nowhere. I found Davison's email and sent him a note. I promised I'd carry a pen and paper with me wherever I went, from that moment on, if he would only tell me where to find this poem. My poet stalking paid off and Davison emailed me back with a note of appreciation and the address of his favorite bookstore. I put down the Neruda and began carrying Peter Davison poems with me.

I was growing tired of responding to personal ads, but I still didn't understand how to meet women in person, so I started emailing another girl I met on the Internet. Kim told me I was funny and brave and it made me feel better that she lived near Laura. I wanted so much, needed so much love and yet couldn't stand for anything to become real. The distance between St. Paul and Brooklyn kept any kind of relationship from actually happening. I went back to dreaming of hugging someone, only this time she had a name.

I called her often. Lying in bed under my grandmother's quilt in the dark, sparse bedroom with only a string of tiny, white lights lining the walls. Kim's voice would come through my rotary phone. I couldn't get enough of her whispers. Her words. After a summer of emails and phone calls, she planned a nine-day vacation to Brooklyn, and I named that fall *The Autumn of the Formerly Decent Woman.*

Kim and I were both nervous when we met at the airport. We took a cab back to my apartment and giggled liked 12-year-olds the entire way. She was exceedingly more cool than I could be and asked if she could lie down for a nap. I followed her into my bedroom and pulled my grandmother's quilt over us both. Her eyes drifted from my lips, to my eyes and then she smiled slowly. I leaned in and we had our first kiss.

Kim had declared herself a lesbian at age 15 and told the world exactly who she was. I wanted to know what that honesty felt like to touch. I kissed her harder. She let me undress her. Her skin was smooth. She kept moving and she was warm. She flushed. I kissed her to make her flush again. She opened her mouth and moaned. I moved under the covers and tasted her. Tasted fierce and real. Tasted how much she needed me. How much she cared for me and wanted me and I gave it to her so she would need it more. We stayed under the quilts and tucked away for her entire vacation. Until Kim had to fly back to St. Paul.

After she left I tried to return to normal by doing laundry and dishes and bills. I forgot to pay the electric bill. The time with Kim made me realize what life could be like. It was like coming in out of the cold and having all your fingers burn back to life. It was hard to wrap my head around the possibilities. There was so much to do, so much that could be done. I wanted to do it all and do it right and do it well to make up for the time lost in my marriage.

I was pleased and proud in my own apartment. I had handed my landlords the first month's rent on Palm Sunday, just before Passover. I can't remember specifically why I chose to move to Brooklyn, except that it seemed easier to get lost in Brooklyn than it would have been to find myself in my parents' Nashville home. The hand of fate on a Palm Sunday. None of that symbolism was lost on me, but I had no way to string it into any kind of divine order. I believed in God, but I didn't know whether or not He believed in me.

I had grown up around Southern Baptists, and while the fundamentalism of my landlords was similar to theirs, the Orthodox Jewish rituals were foreign to me. That fall, my landlords invited me into their Sukkah. The Sukkah is a part of the Jewish celebration of the Sukkot fall, a harvest festival. Jewish families on my block built tiny huts in their backyards and spent time in them to remind themselves of the huts that Moses and the Israelites lived in as they wandered the desert for 40 years.

I sat in my landlords' Sukkah, decorated with fruit and streamers, and they served cookies and laughed when I told them the name of the town where I had grown up. They brought me used furniture when they saw me living with only a couch, an end table, a computer and a pile of cardboard boxes. They reminded me that the daughter in the family was a lawyer "should I need anything," and that they had an extra car, "should I need to go anywhere." Their caring lessened my loneliness. The warmth of their home made my little corner of New York City seem so happy, so wonderful, that there were long nights that I slept with my windows thrown open to Brooklyn, listening to the buses going up and down Kings Highway. Because I felt safe.

I wanted to forget that I was a married woman. That there were legal proceedings surrounding the business of untying my soul from his. When I packed up and moved out, I left him a note that said "in six months, I'll let you know. You should get therapy in the meantime." Six months was up. It was looming over me. I told him six months only because I wanted him to think there was a window. If there was a window, it wasn't truly over. And if it wasn't truly over, then maybe that would temper his rage and keep him from coming after me.

I had spent six years of my life anticipating his rages. I had loved him without being happy about it. I loved how tall and dark he was. His strength. Loved his deep ambition, his desire to get out of Kentucky. I wanted to tap into that, escape those gravel roads with him. I wanted to live in a place with sidewalks and I knew he could get me there. His anger held me. He screamed so loudly, hit so hard, scared me so deeply that I felt. Alive. His curses had given me something to fight against. I got up in the morning to see if I could match him. Outwit him. His rage allowed me to see how strong I was. How much I could endure. I needed his anger to feel alive. I could still be "the good girl" if he was "the bad guy."

His mother sent me a letter a month after I left. She addressed the envelope "Mrs." and told me that her son had some problems, but I needed to uphold my end of the marriage vows. She wrote that he had gone to see a priest and the priest had told him that I was the one in the wrong. The priest said I should have stayed around to work things out. I tore the letter up. Six months after I left, his therapist sent me a letter as well. She wrote that he had been doing well in therapy, but that to really address the issues I would need to go to therapy with him. I was done fixing him, so I tore that letter up, too.

Getting the marriage finalized was coming down to a question of money. A divorce was $1,000 and I didn't have it. I had spent the last of my available credit card balances to buy a bed and put my cat to sleep. And I didn't know if I was ready, because I thought I might still love him. Or did love him. Or at least cared for him. I knew what it was like to hug him. I knew what his hair smelled like after a shower and how it curled around his neck. And I made him cry. I know I did.

That's what hurt. That's what made me stop short when I thought of calling a lawyer. I made him cry and I had a hard time with that. I could skip into the city and play and read and nap. But I broke his heart. I know. He broke mine, too. I know that. I feel that. I live with that. I wanted to be harder. I wanted to be one of those people who could take the big steps without looking back. Without realizing they were tangled up.

I started telling jokes about him. How he didn't know how to tie a tie. He had a job that sometimes called for ties and he would have me tie them for him. I had all of his ties fixed so that he just had to slip them over his head in the mornings and tighten them. While I was packing, I untied all of his ties. I told people jokes using this as a punch line. I pictured him shipping all of his ties back to his mother so she could tie them for him.

I told it as a joke and it made me want to scream. It made me want to yell on street corners,

"I can tie a tie you asshole."

I could. And I could go out to dinner with friends and I could fall in love again. I could hide under quilts in an apartment that was all my own and read poetry. I could have friends and phone calls and visits from family. I could have a Laura Petrie bathroom, landlords who brought me an orange chair for the living room, Al Green blasting on the stereo and cowgirl pictures in my bedroom. I told jokes about ties and I wanted to scream to anyone who would listen, "Screw you. I can have a life. You can take your casserole dishes and the ties and the expectations and the shoulds and coulds and sit in your empty apartment. Sit in that empty apartment alone. Because I. Am Living."

MY CUBICLE at work was where I felt safe. Mega Mega was a global company that had offices in over 100 countries. When I first interviewed at Mega, the department head asked me if I knew what the company did. I had done my homework and delivered what I thought to be a recitation of the company's mission statement from the previous year's annual report. When I finished my speech, she looked at me from behind the desk in her corner office and said, "Actually that's not at all what we do." I still got the job.

Mega Mega was the place where everything made sense and I understood all of the rules. I got bored a lot in my cubicle. I did things to keep myself awake. Sometimes I moved everything. What was on the right side of the desk went left. Even the mouse went over, although it made double-clicking twice as confusing. On the Ides of March, I put a request in the cafeteria's suggestion box that next year they considering having a menu of Caesar Salad and blood pudding. I developed a couple of cubicle-approved jokes that I would throw around. When I came back from lunch I'd say, "I went to McDonald's and I'm totally going to ask for my money back." The unsuspecting coworker would reply, "Why?"

"I got a Happy Meal, and – nothing."

Kim said I had the sense of humor of a Midwestern dad.

My own dad had the sense of humor of a Midwestern dad and I was getting homesick. I wanted to go home. I needed familiar and easy for a change. I was craving Southern accents. The time for the fish fry was rolling around on the calendar. Every year since God was a boy, my dad's hometown had put on a fish fry. A big tent on the fairgrounds, vats of oil, drums of coleslaw and my aunts sitting around talking about who's seeing who and the general state of the world. There was a rodeo. I knew I should hate them but I didn't. I loved it. I loved the hats and the buckles and the boots. I loved the way the guys and girls swaggered around in pressed Wranglers and starched western shirts. I loved sitting in a dirty fairgrounds stand and listening to the rhythm of the conversations. I loved it all, and I needed it more than I'd let on.

My aunt sent me letters from home telling me about taking her wiener dog Buford to the vet. She had eight wiener dogs. She loved those dogs. And she went into great detail about them in the letters I read on my commute.

The letters from home seemed to clash with the world that I had constructed for myself on the D train. I kept track of the quotes I overheard so I could include them in my weekly phone call to my parents. I hoped they'd repeat them to my aunt. I wanted her to understand the world where I read her letters. I told them about the two guys I overheard fighting.

"Lemme 'splain this to you. I wasn't insultin' your mamma. I wasn't insultin' your daddy. I was insultin' you."

I told them about walking past an apartment building on my way home. Two kids started yelling from one of the windows. When I looked up, there were two faces holding up a box of crackers and a sign that read,

Crackers for sale

$1

Peace,

Max

I told them about the morning that an older lady fell, hard, in front of the turnstiles at the Rockefeller Center station. Four hard-core New Yorkers in their Yes-We-Work-At-NBC-And-Don't-We-Look-Great outfits stopped and helped her up.

Helping my aunt to understand my world was an attempt to understand how I had ended up where I had.

I liked pat and dry and easy answers. I had spent 27 years making sure everything fit into a nice little suburban box. I was finding it hard that I didn't fit into a box so easily any more. I kept looking for a "for sure" test. You know, spin around three times, clap your hands and if you start humming the Indigo Girls, then proof positive. Hand that girl a rainbow sticker and tell her to get her hair cut already.

I rolled around with the questions a lot. Am I a real lesbian? Do I really love Kim, or do I just think I do? Am I going to find out later that I'm not lesbian enough and hurt her by falling in love with a man? Am I putting myself through this kind of scrutiny for nothing when in truth I'm straight? I kept wondering, "What if I'm wrong? What if I'm not gay?"

I didn't know what to think. I mean, I had even seen support groups for "lesbians married to men." What the hell did that mean? I couldn't figure out what it meant to be a gay woman. I read every book and magazine I could find. I kept watching movies. I spent far too much money on all the books I bought, but the anarchists took Visa. There were a hell of a lot of those "coming out" stories and all the women in those pages were so sure of their sexuality. Even when they didn't admit it to themselves, they would shoot out answers like, "I always felt different."

What did that mean? Didn't everyone always feel different to some degree? To large degrees? To every degree? Is there anyone who feels the same? That's what I didn't get. I didn't get how it is that you knew for sure.

I asked everyone. I asked Kim, "How'd you know you were gay?"

She just looked at me and said, "Because I fell in love with a woman."

I tried to remember if I had ever really fallen in love with a woman. I had needed Laura and wanted Kim.

I remembered feeling something like love at my eighth-grade graduation dance. The night of the dance, I was looking good. Huge, huge hair that was big and curly. I was taller than almost everyone in my class and I had a fabulous pink dress. I had gone to the dance with my friends. None of us had boyfriends and none of us really cared. We were best friends, the five of us.

As I entered the room I saw her. Amy Purcell. Dancing with her boyfriend. She was slinky, sexy hot. She wasn't popular or known for any slut-like activities. But she was slinky, sexy in a let's-go-for-a-ride-down-by-the-lake-in-a-red-Camaro kind of way. I hit the dance floor and eased up next to her and her boyfriend. I sang into her ear. Amy's eyes flashed. She broke away from her boyfriend and danced with me. When the song ended, Amy Purcell leaned over. In her slinky, sexy in a let's-go-for-a-ride-down-by-the-lake-in-a-red-Camaro kind of way, she whispered in my ear,

"You dance hot."

I wondered if wanting Amy Purcell to notice me made me different.

I pictured Laura and her blue wool coat. I felt the memory of that first of rush of emotion. I wanted to feel that again and I wasn't sure how to get it. Laura would still call me from time to time and apologize for having hurt my feelings. She would say, "I'm sorry" a lot. I told her that she had hurt my feelings more than she could know. I kept picturing us, together. She kept throwing things into the conversation that I didn't know what to do with.

"I want to hold you," she said. I told her I had to hang up.

As much as it made for breathtaking fantasy, I knew that Laura would never translate into reality. I was trying to work on a reality that didn't involve a long-distance relationship. I screwed up the little bit of courage that I had and told Kim that I needed some time to myself. I told myself that meant that I could date other people. I don't remember being incredibly clear with Kim on that particular point. I placed an ad in *The Blade*, one of New York City's gay newspapers, and got two responses. I deleted the first one and arranged to go out for coffee with Roxanne. She wore a flannel shirt over a white t-shirt and asked me a lot about myself.

I didn't tell Kim any of it and I told myself there was nothing wrong with what I was doing.

I was jittery and anxious in the days leading up to the one-year anniversary of leaving my marriage. I was planning to spend the week in Minnesota with Kim. I hadn't told her all there was to know about my seeing someone else. I had twice gone out for coffee with Roxanne and I told Kim she was just a friend. I left out the fact that she was a friend I happend to meet when she answered my personal ad in the back of *The Blade*. I told myself that nothing had happened and if it did, I would tell Kim.

The day of my flight, I decided to skip lunch and leave work at 4:30. I would take the subway to 125th Street and determine from there if I thought the bus would get me to the airport on time. If not, I'd take a cab. I was nervous. I wanted everything to go well.

Kim had made plans for us to stay at a retreat center run by nuns in the middle of the state. It was the same night that just a year earlier, I had left my husband. It snowed and I kept calling the ground "tundra." The nuns gave us our own domed cabin. It was made of pine wood and had quilts scattered throughout. There was a fire raging in the fireplace. We spent the night lying on the floor, and talking. I told her I needed more. I pulled her up into the loft next to the skylights. An ice storm raged outside and I pulled her clothes off. Her breasts were larger than I remembered. I buried my head in them. She flushed and moved her thighs in between mine. I clamped my legs together and tried to hold her in place and bit her neck to make her stay. Ice collected in the window above us and I moved my hand inside her. She threw her head back and moaned. I wanted to make her mine. Make her stay. Make her follow me back to Brooklyn. She shivered and fell beside me. She gathered her clothes and moved to the bed downstairs to sleep. She whispered, "It's too hot here next to you."

The next day I went to see Laura. Kim dropped me off at the campus where she was teaching. Laura took me back to her apartment and pulled out some pictures to show me. She knelt down beside me to flip through them. I stared at her thighs. Her strong thighs. She saw where my eyes landed and stood up. She told me I had nice jeans. She put her hands on my hips to see them closer. I told her it was too late for that. She told me she never wanted to have sex with me anyway. She held my waist and said, "I'll miss you even more when you're gone." Kim came back and took me to the airport. I flew home to New York and tried to remember how to keep control of my life.

When I was young, religion had given my life some structure. But I stopped going to mass after I left the marriage. I couldn't walk into a Catholic church without crying.

Religion and the spirit and God had always been in my life in one way or another. I had grown up the Catholic girl around friends who attended Southern Baptist and Church of Christ congregations. It was expected that the family Bible would be set out on the coffee table wrapped, more often than not, in a quilted covering someone had made in Sunday School.

I spent the summers of my childhood riding up and down the gravel roads of Kentucky in a faded blue VW Bug. Four of us kids and Claudine would pile into her car and try to outrun the heat trapped in her doublewide. It was the same miserable route every day. Sweaty legs sticking to the seat and to each other, we'd ride past the Dairy Dip down to the lake. We'd head along the river, then out to the old abandoned Coke plant. A cloud of dust would trail out behind us and come into the car to plaster itself on our faces. We'd circle around at the dead end where the bridge had washed out long before I was even a thought. We kept the windows rolled down and we'd drink our 16-ounce bottles of Coke and Claudine would sing to us.

Claudine was my mom's age and lived next door. My dad always called her "ma'am" and took off his work cap when he stepped into her place to pick us up. Claudine once told me he was the most polite man she'd ever met. My dad told us that we should be extra careful to not be a bother to Claudine on account of that husband and two kids of hers. We'd listen because we always listened to my dad and we'd listen to Claudine. Because Claudine could sing. She could sing "Coal Miner's Daughter" better than Loretta could. She'd sing Patsy Cline so hard it'd make me cry for reasons I couldn't figure out. We'd go up and down every back road within reach and we'd roll down the windows, throw our arms out to catch the wind and Claudine would sing.

Claudine was the one who made sure I got saved. She knew me and my sister were Catholic and she didn't mind. She knew that we thought we had been saved in our own way, but she just wanted to make sure everything took. The summer I was 12, Claudine invited us to a revival at the First Assembly of God. One of the rules of Claudine's church was that girls had to wear dresses. That left my sister out. So on the promise of free cotton candy and an RC Cola, I went with Claudine to the revival in her VW Bug. She sang Dolly Parton's "Coat of Many Colors" on the way over. I drank my RC.

The Assembly of God didn't look anything like St. Mary's. Dark wood paneling lined the walls and a giant painted mural of Jesus sitting on a rock petting a blonde kid's head was up at the front of the room. The walls were painted mauve to match the cushions on the pews and the carpet was a soft blue. It looked like someone's living room.

I wish I could remember all of what was said that night. I wish I could remember what it was exactly that got me down on my knees with my eyes shut tight and my hands clamped around one another. I remember a man at the front of the room, I remember his name was Brother Steve. I remember him telling a story about a woman he had visited a couple of months back, out at the trailer park. She had been a hairdresser and had never been saved. Never wanted Jesus in her life. I remember him saying that he sat with her and told her about the Lord and all He could do for her. And she cried and he cried and she wanted more than anything to have Jesus in her heart. But she didn't want to do it right then. She wanted to wait a week so she could go to church and go up front and do it right with her kids and grandkids around her. Brother Steve said he tried to talk her out of it. Said that she should ask Jesus in her heart right then and there. But she wouldn't do it.

The next week there was a car accident and that woman died. She died without having called Jesus into her heart and she went to hell. She went to spend an eternity in the flames of the pit because she had wanted to wait. Brother Steve asked if we wanted to make sure that didn't happen to us. He asked if we wanted to burn in hell like that or spend eternity in the loving embrace of Our Lord and Savior. He asked if we wanted Jesus to come into our hearts and fill us to overflowing with life everlasting.

I felt my neck flush and my knees start to tremble and all I could do was whisper "yes... yes... yes..." to every one of Brother Steve's questions. I felt Claudine's hand on my back and heard the whole church singing the "come forward" song. And Brother Steve was saying if we wanted Jesus in our hearts. If we wanted Him in our souls. If we wanted that love everlasting, we should come forward and have his hand laid on us. And the church was singing and I felt my neck flush and my knees tremble and all I could hear was Claudine's strong voice singing.

And I went. I went forward because it all seemed so sure. I did want that love. I did want that rush that power that fullness that Brother Steve was calling forward. I wanted so hard to make the world feel that solid forever. And I didn't want Claudine to stop singing for me. So I went. Brother Steve asked if I was sure about loving Jesus. I whispered "yes" and he laid his hand on me and said that I was saved.

I went everywhere in New York City trying to recapture that feeling. I had lost it in the Catholic church, and I tried to reclaim it in other places. I found the Quaker meeting in Brooklyn and traveled an hour and a half each Sunday by bus and by subway to sit there in silence. I rarely stayed to talk to anyone afterward. Sometimes I would drift downstairs after the meeting and silently sit in on the Peace and Social Justice Committee meetings. I was looking for a way to understand the "whys." Why floods? Why hurricanes? Why the Holocaust and AIDS and why the really bad commute? I wanted to know why I had gotten married and gotten hit. I wanted something beyond "It's the will of God." I wanted to understand "why" and I craved the silence of the Brooklyn Quakers.

I was obsessed with religion and God and love and sex. I needed hobbies. Inner resources. Outside interests. I spent so much headspace on relationships. I thought it might be silly to be thinking about love so much.

My friend Rachel and her husband moved to New York from Tucson that winter and everything changed. We had become fast friends on our road trip to Montreal, and I loved that I finally had a relationship in my life that didn't involve plane trips or long-distance phone calls. We made the most of it.

One morning Rachel called and told me to meet her at Flatbush Plaza. She needed to buy a couch. We giggled through the showroom as Lenny the salesman showed us sofas. Lenny told us his life story.

He told us about his house in Mill Basin. He liked his house but he wanted to "get the fuck outta Brooklyn." He was looking at some property in Florida next month. Lenny showed us a couch with a coffee table that pulled up to be a TV tray. I told Lenny, "That would be great for watchin' the game."

Lenny looked at my Yankees sweatshirt and said, "You're damn right it would be." After Rachel pulled out her credit card for the sofa and loveseat, Lenny said, "I like you two. You're funny."

We went out to the Rising to celebrate everything, so we went to the Rising to celebrate the new furniture. The Rising was a lesbian bar at the corner of Rachel's street. We discussed queer theories and why it was that her black nephew-in-law wanted to be known as "Chocolate Cher." We downed pints and she listened to me repeat over and over,

"I can't believe I really left my husband. I can't believe I'm really sitting in a lesbian bar. Do you know where I was last year? Do you know what I was doing last year? I'll tell you one thing. I wasn't hanging out in the Rising and talking to Lenny at the furniture store in Marine Park."

In the course of speaking of capitalism and all things good, Rachel mentioned that she was going to go through her clothes and throw some out. Apparently "throwing some out" meant passing them along to someone who could use them. Someone who had a strict, five-page dress code to maintain in the workplace and no money to maintain it with. Someone like me. My credit had been wrecked by my husband's habit of charging everything that caught his eye. His insistence that we live in Manhattan meant that I had to get cash advances on my credit cards to pay the rent. Any time I balked, he would scream, "fat, lazy, bitch" and I would give in. I needed new clothes and Rachel's old ones would do just fine. She let me go through her bag of discards and I took nearly everything. I wandered back home with my homeless woman-looking bag. Dragging it onto two buses and the D train to get from her apartment to mine.

I had always struggled for money. Even after we married, when we should have had enough, my husband spent far more than we earned and we had more bills than we could pay. He once had me get tested to see if I could sell my eggs to a fertility clinic. He heard we could get $5,000 for them. He decided that two donations would solve all of our problems.

Every morning for a week, I traveled over a hundred blocks uptown to undergo a battery of physical and psychological evaluations. They told me I would have to stick myself with needles for weeks in order to grow the eggs. They claimed it was a simple outpatient procedure to extract the eggs once they were ready.

In the end, I was turned down because my mother had a history of cataracts.

He wasn't happy and I was left with the feeling that I could never have enough money or make enough money. I kept it in the back of my mind that I could always sell my body parts if I needed to. I knew how to lie about the history of cataracts so that I could make it happen if I needed the cash.

I started drinking Jack Daniels and Coke at night after work. Even with Rachel's donated clothes, I had nothing to wear to work and my morning coffee was perpetually lukewarm. I got a series of emails from my mother asking why I wasn't coming to visit more often. My boss kept yelling at me because the car service picking him up parked on the opposite side of the building and the department head told me I should have made him take the subway anyway. I felt powerless, and on top of everything, my boss wanted to take my name off the magazine I had been editing on my own for over a month. I believed in karma, but I told myself none of this had anything to do with the fact that I had slept with someone else before totally breaking it off with Kim.

The next day I realized that the magazine was going to be late and a little slapped-together looking. It would do well to have someone else's name stuck on it. I told the boss he should list me as "Production Editor." He fell for it and I felt back in control.

I went home. The next day was the Mermaid Parade at Coney Island and I wanted to be ready.

The Mermaid Parade was one of the bawdiest rites of summer passage that the world as I knew it offered. People walked down the streets around Coney Island dressed in exotic costumes that were barely-there. There was a small parade of cars and mermaids and as much nakedness as the NYPD would let them get away with. It happened every year, and I wasn't going to miss this one. I couldn't persuade anyone to go with me, so I boarded the D train by myself. When we rounded the bend by the ocean and caught sight of the water, all the small girls on the train dressed as mermaids squealed with delight. I did too. The conductor announced, "Next stop Coney Island…the Land of the Rising Sun!" We all giggled.

We weren't disappointed. Surrounded by people in body glitter, ribbons, sparkles, rhinestones and women without tops, the cops in blue just looked out of it. Like they grated against the cotton candy energy everyone else had going on. I grabbed a lemonade, sat down on the curb and took it all in. Took in all the garish decay of the freak shows lining the boardwalk. People strolling around with candy apples speaking a million different languages and arty, black-clad Manhattanites who traveled out for the day. There were families with matriarchs in tow repeating the phrase, "when I was a kid…" I sat on the curb and soaked it in.

The Mermaid Parade had been scheduled for the same day as the Dyke March. I had never been to the annual march down Fifth Avenue. I didn't understand the politics of it and I didn't intend to go. I especially didn't intend to go by myself, but I found myself back on the train and heading into the city. I wanted to see what a parade of dykes looked like. I wanted to see if any of them looked like me. I wanted to see if I could make myself fit into the parade. The train stopped at Park Slope, three couples got on and they all nodded and smiled at me.

When I got off the train at Bryant Park, I stopped short. It was filled with lesbians. There was a large group of older dykes in leather beating drums. Everyone seemed to know everyone else. I walked around with my mouth hanging open. There was a girl in a white tank top with long, blonde hair, red lipstick and a cowboy hat. She kept laughing and shooting her friends with a water pistol. I followed her around the park and the drums got louder. The group stepped off onto Fifth Avenue and I stayed behind the girl in the hat. She kept laughing and I realized we had walked ten blocks. It was hot and it seemed too much trouble to step out of the group. People stood on the side of the streets and clapped.

The girl in the cowboy hat would run up to her friends and kiss them. I kept getting handed leaflets for Dyke Nights. The girl in the cowboy hat ran over to a boy who looked like the boys I grew up with. The boys with the big, silver rodeo belts and the Levi's swagger. I looked closer and realized that boy hadn't been born a boy and it shocked me a bit. The girl in the cowboy hat planted a kiss on the boy's cheek and ran off. I stood in the middle of Fifth Avenue and let them walk past me. A group of gay men held up signs that read, "Brothers Love Sisters" and I kept walking. It seemed the right thing to do. I wanted to see where the girl in the cowboy hat went. I wanted to figure out how she did it. How she moved so easily and how she had made her friends. I wanted to move that easily. I wanted to run and kiss strangers. I wanted to walk in the NYC Dyke March, so I kept moving and walked from Bryant Park to Washington Square. And I realized. I realized without a doubt. That I wasn't the only one.

I WAS sitting around the apartment and realized something had to be done. My apartment had not been made fully a home. Emotionally it provided, but physically the place hadn't really come together yet. My voice was bouncing off the bedroom walls and that was just wrong. I hung up posters. I went to Chinatown, where I uncovered some vintage-looking advertisements with Chinese lesbians smoking cigarettes. I went to the home center place down by my train station and got a curtain rod. I got a toilet scrub brush, some Comet and ant killer. I hung the curtain rod along one of the bedroom walls, and set it up to display the quilt my grandmother made for my 16th birthday. My grandmother's quilts were such an everyday part of my life that I forgot not everyone has them. I have the baby quilt she made me. It's quite worn — I carried it everywhere with me. I have an in-between quilt, which I cherish because it's made from all the baby doll clothes my sister and I played with. It's also the same fabric that had been my dad's and aunts' play clothes.

I was just starting to learn how to cherish those quilts. I didn't have really great memories of my grandmother. I wish I did. She constantly accused me of being too fat. She told me I didn't stand up for myself. She told me I was too much of a pushover. I think she was bitter. I think she got hard. I think maybe she put whatever was left into those quilts.

I planned a trip home to Nashville. The land of the fried food accent and mom hugs and this was good. My sister called to tell me that the Bass beers I bought when I was there at Christmas were still in the fridge. Apparently my dad could go out and buy more Budweiser, but he wasn't touching my Bass. For years my dad had spent his weekends drinking more than he should. It was something that none of us talked about because we didn't want to make it any more real than it already was. We told ourselves that since he drank only on the weekends, it didn't count. I wonder if that's what he told himself, too.

It was always weird to be back in Nashville. I kept forgetting that I couldn't comment too often on how totally hot Ashley Judd was. I wanted to have that conversation with them someday. I wanted to be the good little rainbow activist. I figured I'd let their last check for the divorce clear before I laid another thing on them. "Oh hi mom. My husband beat me. I left him. I'm getting a divorce. I'm not going to mass. And, by the way, I'm a dyke."

I missed New York the second the plane landed in Nashville. My sister took me shopping. I bought used CDs from a kid with twelve piercings and green hair. I wanted to run up to him and scream, "I'm one of you! Seriously! Take me to your bar!" Instead I bought my BR5-49, Dolly Parton, kd lang and Loretta Lynn. I went to Red Lobster for dinner with the family. My mom loved the kd lang I played for her.

While I was South, I took a trip back to Possum Trot. My parents had moved to Nashville around the time my younger sister graduated from high school. My mother was done living in the country and she wanted more. She took my dad with her. I wanted to see what Possum Trot looked like after having lived in New York, so I made them drive the two hours to see it with me. It wasn't quaint like my memories. The Dairy Dip wasn't cute and the economy wasn't humming. The biggest form of entertainment still appeared to be riding three-wheelers down the main highway and it's still such that you have to know the waitress at the barbeque place personally in order to get your sweet tea returned for the unsweet tea you originally ordered.

The Republican Party had set up a big storefront in the town where the old folks still remembered how TVA and the New Deal brought electricity and running water to a part of the world that wouldn't have had it otherwise. The local paper still featured wedding pictures of kids who graduated from high school that year. The place wasn't run down, either. There were nice houses and nice SUVs. The ball fields were well-kept and kids were the highest priority.

But I felt more "outside" than ever driving through that town. I couldn't wait to get out. I felt claustrophobic and trapped and generally like I didn't belong, which I never did. It's a great place for those who do belong. It was a great place for those who pray to the right God and have the right family. It's a great place for those who don't really mind the Republicans and who are friendly with the guy who wrote the anti-choice letter to the editor.

I had a hard time seeing how I got from there to a job in midtown Manhattan. I stared at the one-lane road I used to live on. I stared at the house I grew up in.

It had been different when we were young. When we were young, my sister and I existed on the banks of the Tennessee River. We owned the summers when we were girls. We ran wild through humid summer days that never ended and only melted one into the other. We floated down rivers of weekdays with no school, no rules, no parents and no constructs other than our fantasies. We were good girls my sister and I. We had nothing to rebel against. This was life as we knew it and we knew the summers to be long and to be ours.

After our parents had pulled out of the driveway and gone to work, I'd go out every morning to check the mail. I'd watch for the mail lady to pull up to our box and put in our envelopes. On the days when I had put in a mason jar lid with just enough change to obtain stamps for contacting the outside world, it would take her a bit longer to pull away from our mailbox. I hated that I had bothered her and made her job longer. I liked that she knew that someone in our house sent letters into the outside world.

I liked walking to the mailbox in my bare feet and leaving footprints on the dewy grass. I imagined that feeling the wetness on the bottom of my feet made me a poet somehow. I had never read poetry, outside of some Emily Dickinson. But I knew that poets and poems and words strung together existed, and I imagined that people who knew of such things would walk to their mailbox through the morning dew in their bare feet.

Our neighbors lived in doublewide trailers set up on cinder blocks, or in small ranch houses like ours. We shared a party line phone service and not much else with our next-door neighbors. We listened in to one another's conversations. Their boy once threw tomatoes at our picture window. We stole all his Fisher Price toys. The house across the street was set back from the road and hidden by trees and the honeysuckle vines that we would pick clean while waiting for the school bus. We could hear the boy who lived in that house racing around his yard in endless circles in a go-kart. His dad once bought a goat to avoid cutting the lawn. We didn't know what to make of any of this, but we developed intricate plans of faked friendship with that boy in order to get to drive that go-kart ourselves.

Our summers were endless and they were all ours. We planned our weddings with the help of Barbie and the tiny, purple wildflowers growing in our side yard. We became scientists and tested concoctions of milk, orange juice and mouthwash. We liked to add enough liquids to cause the concoctions to bubble. When we ran out of sweets to eat, we snitched Flintstone vitamins out of the medicine cabinet for our sugar rush. We ate handfuls of bittersweet chocolate chips and licked peanut butter off spoons. We mastered Kraft Macaroni and Cheese for our lunches and we dutifully called our mother at work three times a day to let her know what we were up to.

We constructed our summer days into our own shape away from the prying eyes of any adults. We sneaked copies of our dad's *Playboys* and charged the neighbor boys to view them. We made crank calls around the county telling people they had won a new car. "What kind?" they'd ask. "Red" we'd say. We'd always say red. We'd put on our mom's old prom dresses complete with gloves and hats and sing back-up to the C.W. McCall song "Convoy" that we found on our dad's turntable. We went on hikes into the woods behind our house. Under barbed-wire fences and through tangled undergrowth. Heat and humidity finding its way through the leaves of the trees and onto our flushed faces. We waded in the streams we were always surprised to come across. We walked past the cars and auto parts that had been abandoned beyond any road that we knew to be through those woods. We'd reach the edge of the tree line and come out unexpectedly into a cow pasture. Perch on the gate. Or stretch out on the large, flat limestone rock that marked the end of the woods behind our house.

And one day. During a thunderstorm that had blown up along the Tennessee River. One of those storms that make the day go dark and the humidity blow away. Electricity in the air and the sharp crispness of a summer being blown wide open. The air goes still and quiet with a pink glow before the winds rush in. We one day during a summer thunderstorm like that, threw open all the doors and windows to the house. We found the classical station from two towns away on the radio and we cranked up the speakers. We turned up the bass. We let the wind blow in and churn our summer day around. We let the thump of the music we were only vaguely familiar with rattle the window panes. And we twirled.

We twirled wearing prom dresses and taffeta and lace. We twirled in the living room in the wind in the music – through the summer. We twirled and we imagined that we were poets and dancers and scientists and spring brides. We twirled and imagined that if we let it in. If we let in the thunder, the storm, the wind and the music. If we could throw open the doors to that house on the banks of the Tennessee River and let in the world. Then we imagined that we could live in our summers. When we were girls.

I flew back to New York and tried to return to the safety of my cubicle, but Possum Trot was always there. On the way into work, I made a woman uncomfortable on the subway. I felt horrible about it. I didn't mean to, and as soon as it happened, I felt my heart sink into my stomach. The woman got on the train and she was dressed pretty much like the rest of us. But I could tell she was totally working class, see how she made-do. She was wearing a child's belt. I stared at it without even thinking. I must have been obvious. She self-consciously pulled her jacket around, over her belt. She didn't look directly at me, but she looked embarrassed.

I wanted to tell her I was sorry. That she was beautiful and who cares about belts anyway. That she was a lovely and gorgeous person and please don't let a random stranger staring on a train embarrass you.

I thought about the first temp job I had after I moved to New York. It was at Calvin Klein Cosmetics in the Trump Tower at 57th Street. The one next to Tiffany's and across from The Plaza. And let me just state for the record, that the clothes that receptionists in Nashville wear. Clothes that were purchased on a mighty annual salary of $18,000, are not the appropriate clothes for walking into the Trump Tower. Even if you're not entirely sure what clothes are appropriate for the Trump Tower, you know that when you're wearing clothes purchased at a strip mall in a Kentucky town with a population of 3,000, you shouldn't walk into the Trump Tower and try to pass yourself off as an executive assistant to the director of advertising for Calvin Klein Cosmetics. Even if you are just a temp.

But what the hell choice did I have? I was already saying the wrong things and speaking with the wrong accent and they. All the "theys" from Long Island or Westchester or wherever it was that "they" were from. They all stared and laughed a bit and raised an eyebrow when I pulled a peanut butter and jelly sandwich out of the backpack I had bought for $10 at KMart. I tried. I desperately tried not to cry because I needed that job.

I realized only recently that girl was gone. I had learned how to move with "those people." I had learned to hide the Southern accent and to buy bargain clothes that still looked New York. I had gotten a new haircut, a good job and I never carried my lunch in a paper bag. But I still felt out of place.

 chapter

7

I AM here to testify.

I am here to testify. That when they say, you can have it all, be whatever you want to be, whoever you want to be, be yourself, be your dream, be your vision of whirled peace. Grab a piece of the pie, reach for the sky, pull yourself up by your boot straps, by your belt straps, by your strapping youth. That it's a rags-to-riches tale on the order of the American dream, with side orders of baseball, apple pie, mom and Chevrolet in any order you like. I am here to testify that. They do not mean it.

I am here. I am here to testify that when they mouth the words, "You can be anything you want to be" to small schoolchildren in the outpost of Western Kentucky, otherwise known as Possum Trot. (Cue Yankee laugh-track here.) They do not mean it. They. They hang the Ten Commandments on the wall. The Ten Commandments of the Southern Baptist version in every classroom from kindergarten to high school and fail to mention what consequences lie with a lay in the back seat of your daddy's Chevrolet at the drive-in down by the lake. They fail to mention the power of the Ivy League on the resume. And the circle my friends. Remains unbroken.

I am here. I am here to testify. I am here to testify that when they say *New York's streets are lined with gold.* They fail to mention the first month's, last month's, security deposit plus broker's fee, credit check, double-check, paycheck, W-2s, in-state references, bank references and bankable assets required to rent that U-haul and become part of the Hampton subset. There are no parents to bankroll this foolishness, no trust funds no savings bonds no pennies in jars to put under these castles in the air. Nor under these tenements in the city.

I am here. I am here to testify. I am here to testify that when they say *reach for the stars.* They fail to factor in pink-collar ghettos, the glass ceiling the nights working until 8 and a boss who mentions the time when the cubicle is reached at ten past 9. They fail to mention the hour-and-a-half commute one way for those who can't afford to live closer to those steel skyscrapers. They fail to mention that a 40-hour work week factored by a boss of two, divided by meals cooked and consumed alone, always alone, multiplied by a commute to the outer borough's outer reaches and factored with a degree of sheer exhaustion. That this. Leaves no room beyond becoming a cog. There are no flights of fancy or daydreams of rhinestones.

I am here. I am here to testify. I am here to testify that when they say, *Why is she with him? Is she stupid? Doesn't she know any better? Isn't she pitiful, stringy haired, bruised and ugly?* They fail to see. Fail. Utterly and totally and completely. To see. Who the victim is here. She. She is not stupid. She knows better. She. I'll tell you. I am here to testify that she does not enjoy waking to bruises to blood to tears and to threats. I am here to testify to the sheer energy required to pack the boxes and the spices, hire the movers, find the apartment, map Brooklyn, put down deposits obtain a post office box, emergency cell phone, change of address forms and solo checking account. Pull money from the air, divide the debts, divide the assets, divide the forms, make copies, make phone calls. Cry. A lot. And obtain the pile of cash that the world deems necessary in *Circumstances Such As These.* To match that steely determination.

I am here. I am here to testify.
To the power of. One.
I am here. I am. One.
Human.

chapter 8

MY FRIENDS Kevin and Lisa came up from Baltimore to visit for the weekend. The spring was warm and light and I was falling in love with the city and I wanted to introduce them to all the places and things I had uncovered. We went to Coney Island and walked the boardwalk with cotton candy in hand. Hawkers were yelling through megaphones that if you knocked over three milk bottles, you could win a "prayer bear." We counted more Puerto Rican flags than Haitian. We drank lemonade and watched the Cyclone taking 90-degree turns.

We went into the city and found my favorite Persian restaurant. I hadn't been there in two years, but the waiter remembered I liked the chicken kabobs with the cucumber yogurt on the side. We walked from there to the Tonic at Norfolk and Houston. A girl I knew was in a band that was having a CD launch party. She played the electric cello and she signed my CD.

The next day I met up with Rachel and went into Times Square to see a Broadway show. Afterward, we took over a sidewalk table at an Italian restaurant in the West Village and we laughed at the tourists as they walked by. It was spring and it was warm and I couldn't remember a time when I had smiled so much. When I had been surrounded by so many friends and I could walk through the city with as much freedom as I now knew I had.

I was enjoying the freedom and I was letting little things drop. I kept forgetting to buy light bulbs. My landlord needed me to have a key made for the front door and I couldn't remember to do it. I found a diner near my apartment that would sell me French toast and link sausages for two dollars. The waitress kept calling me "hon." I decided that the cat I had recently adopted was the best thing in my life because she loved me unconditionally. I compiled a mental check-list of the people I loved so that I could go through it on my morning commutes. It calmed my nerves to remember how and who to love. The last name on my list was New York City. In addition to Alice the cat, it was the one thing that was always there for me. Bright lights, big city and concrete fraying around the edges. It was all mine and it was always there when I needed it. I had lived in the city for four years, and I was just realizing I loved it.

One night, I stayed out too late drinking and slept at Rachel's. She outfitted me the next day in khaki Capri pants and a blue oxford shirt. No fewer than three people at work commented on how casually I was dressed. I told them, "I thought it was summer." My boss said, "I thought we had a five-page dress code."

That night Roxanne and I went to see an angst-ridden-queer, racial, message-of-homelessness theater production. The entire night I felt very much like a Gap ad set down in the middle of a Greenwich Village queer center. Rachel's husband told me that I was both an 80-year-old woman who was bitter and cynical about life, and a 16-year-old girl sitting in her bedroom, never been kissed. The theater made me feel 16, Midwestern and straight. On the way home, the bus driver yelled after me as I stepped off the bus, "You gotta put the pedal to the metal!"

I stood in the middle of Kings Highway and laughed. I had no idea what he meant by that, but it was something my dad had always told me. He told me phrases while I was learning to drive. A string of phrases that seemed to lead one into the other. "Put the pedal to the metal. Keep it between the ditches. It takes a good driver to hit all the potholes." I wondered if the driver of the B82 taught his kids to drive in an endless string of Southern sayings.

At work, I had fallen in love with my graphic designer. I had no idea what she looked like. She worked for another company and I sent her my articles to lay out in the company magazine. She fixed the fonts and placed my words in 32 pages of regular columns on glossy paper. She searched her files for stock photos that made my articles about corporate oversight look like something I would want to read. She called me on the phone from time to time and asked me if I had seen her galleys yet.

She asked me if we had ever considered a magazine devoted solely to shareholder haiku. She told me that we should print a blank magazine that would be mailed to all 50,000 Mega-workers around the globe and call the entire thing a "Dada approach to employee communications." I told her she needed her own design firm. I told her, "You need to nurture your inner prom queen. Chances are she'll turn all Carrie on you, but you still get the crown. And that's really all that matters." She laughed and told me in that gorgeous, awesome voice of hers, "You're hilarious, you know." I twirled my desk chair around, wrapping the phone cord tight against my body and wanted to yell, "I love you!" It came out in a giggly, high-pitched voice that said only, "I'll fax those proofs right over." I told her I was sending her flowers when we got the issue out. She told me I should come over to her office to proof my blues in person.

Proofing my blues in person seemed a fine idea. Because while the freedom of my days spent in the company of friends and co-workers was intoxicating, the nights spent alone in my head were excruciating. I told myself the city was enough for me. That I didn't need anyone or anything other than phone calls to an unseen graphic designer. It didn't work. I spent all of my energy being happy during the day and I had nothing left over at night. I sat in my pink tub and wondered what it would be like if I were to finally kick the radio over the edge with a peach floral-scented, bubble-bathed toe. I wondered what would happen if I went to the 24-7 CVS Pharmacy across the street and purchased pink body glitter and rust-proof razor blades. I thought about lying in the tub under the disco ball I had hung from the shower and drawing that razor down my vein.

I could taste that dark void and the free fall down to the metal and skin and I stopped. I stopped wondering because I realized. That I didn't want anyone at Mega Mega to know. I didn't want any of my friends to see the turmoil. I didn't want anyone to know that I hurt.

My reputation at Mega Mega was important to me. I worked hard. I contributed. I was respected. And I learned a lot there. Most recently, I had learned that no matter how tightly you clench your jaw, you cannot will the head of communications to return your phone call. The second I *finally* heard his booming Southern accent on the phone, I got movement back in my face. I had needed him to call me and and approve the articles for publishing. His was the last phone call I needed and the waiting drove me insane. I had pulled out my entire bag of corporate communications tricks on this guy.

His title made him too important for me to call directly to ask him to get his butt in gear. Instead, I called his assistant and sweetly said, "Would you mind asking Mr. Boss Man over there to read his articles?" A week later it becomes, "Would you mind giving Mr. Boss Man over there a little nudge?" Sometimes I would take matters into my own hands, sneak into the building two hours before the administrative assistants arrived and lay my memo on top of the Boss Man's in-box. In the end, none of those worked. I had to have my boss call his boss. Sometimes it's the old-fashioned org chart that works best.

I found out that a person who had been offered one of the open positions in the department had turned it down. I found out they had offered her $85,000 for one of the jobs I was doing. It was almost double my salary even with the recent raise and I tried to ignore it. Instead of complaining, I called the cable company. I had been living without proper television for too long. I had been trying to save money since I moved out of the marriage, and had been living on the three channels my television could pull out of the air.

While I had to rely on this virtual escape, my boss took a week's vacation into the wilds of the Southwest. I hoped he'd get a little too close to that canyon out there. Our ad rep called and nearly started crying when he realized the boss was out.

"Can I help you, Scott?" I asked.

"God I hope so."

The week the boss chose to take off was what we in the world of cubicles would call a "crucial week." Earnings were released that week and two of our biggest publications were going to press. Two of the editors in the department had quit or transferred out and it was all left for me, the assistant editor in the hand-me-down clothing, to handle. I sat down over beers with Rachel and drafted a memo to the boss requesting a "job/salary restructuring." I had been collecting terms people had recently used to describe me. I had "dramatic," "life in tumult" and "high-energy." I looked over the list and wondered why it was that most nights I was sitting at home playing Nintendo. I used none of those descriptions in the memo to the boss. I determined that the boss was an idiot on a massive level. "Crucial weeks" at the very least require "face time" which is hard to achieve when one is on a burro in Arizona.

We had written the memo at a two-for-one night and the next day at Mega Mega was my annual "Take Our Children To Work Day" presentation. I hadn't gotten home until midnight and at one point I was so drunk that my gums were numb. I had managed to spend an obscene amount of money. I had a theory that every time you went into Manhattan, they should just take $80 out of your pocket. I figured we could cut out a lot of time and middlemen if the City of New York just took the money up front and handed you two drink tickets and a voucher for a cab ride as you crossed the river.

I pulled off the presentation to 15 kids while staring at them through red, glazed-over eyes. I avoided explaining to the kiddies the pitfalls of going out to a two-for-one on a school night. I had them write fake press releases about one another. They moaned and sighed at the idea of having to write anything. I avoided saying "Yeah, get cracking you whiners." I tried to make it fun. I told them that interviewing someone was just like gossiping and they took to it like ducks to water. On the way out, I heard four of them say, "That was really fun." I went into a bathroom, shut the stall door and took a nap.

My salary restructuring memo made it to the boss on plantain day. Each week, going through the cafeteria line, one of the servers would look up at me and say, "If it's Thursday, it must be plantain day!" I never knew what to make of that, but I always got an order from him. I knew he was from Michigan and I wanted to bond with someone who was from somewhere else, too. Plus he mixed up an incredibly nice baked sole with watercress vinaigrette. I was proud of the memo. Instead of going into great detail about second-hand clothes and doing the jobs of three people, I had written:

When you have a moment, I'd like to set up a time to discuss with you some of the extra responsibilities I've taken on over the last few months, and look at ways to shape those into a more appropriate job structure and compensation package. I'd like to move into a position that has an editorial focus on electronic communications — including the Web site and intranet — and also be considered for the editor's responsibilities.

My boss took two weeks to get back to me. He gave me a $5,000 raise and a new title. He still had me make lunch reservations for him and he still yelled at me every time the heat in his office wasn't working well.

Someone asked me if I thought the glass was half empty or half full. I realized that I worried a lot that there was no glass at all. But somewhere inside, I was firmly convinced that the glass was half-full. I needed to get a life. Obtain a purpose. Stop talking to the cat. Stop pounding the keyboard on the Internet and step out of the apartment now and then. I called Kim and told her I could never be a Mets fan because they were an expansion team.

I didn't tell her that I had gone on another date with Roxanne.

Roxanne and I went to see a documentary at the Quad Cinemas and I knew the second she brushed up against me. I knew when her arm drifted over just a bit. I knew after dinner when she asked me if I wanted to come over. I knew I wouldn't be going home anytime soon.

When she asked me, I nodded yes.

We watched a good half hour of a rented movie and she pulled me to her. Her hands drifted down and under and over and God. In. Her hands drifted in.

Jesus.

She pulled my shirt up and my skirt down. She kept whispering. She whispered how it felt. How she felt. How I felt.

"Put your leg on my shoulder."

All I could do was moan. And flush.

Jesus.

"Tell me where you feel it."

The things she did. Her thighs, her arms. So strong and she rode me.

"Do you like that?"

She touched me and licked me. For hours. And we fell asleep until I woke again with her hands and her mouth.

"God you're insatiable. Yes."

The next day Roxanne drove me to Rachel's apartment so I could feed her cats while she and her husband were away. Roxanne let me out and drove off without a kiss goodbye. I told myself I shouldn't have expected one.

We went to the movies again and didn't get home until 2 a.m. Roxanne had asked me back to her apartment and I went because I was intrigued with the things that she did. I was obsessed with the things she had me do. I couldn't stop thinking about the words she had me say.

I would find myself whispering "please" for days after.

There had been a summer breeze drifting through an open window. I sank down and into and through myself and around the tangled sheets of her bed. I glimpsed a green-hued digital clock inching toward dawn. I caught the sounds of neighbors coming home from a night out. Sirens. Police sirens, ambulance sirens, fire engine sirens. A whirring black metal fan. There were crisp linens bunched around my thighs, my toes digging down into the folds and there were her hands. Her hands wrapped around my waist pulling me close. Her breath on my back. Her hot breath on the small of my neck and I felt the heat rise up in a flush. Closed my eyes to steady the swirl of emotions. Skin on skin, her chest moved against mine. A black whirring metal fan. Cats meowing in another room. A summer breeze drifted in through open Brooklyn windows. There were simply hands and fingers and touches. Her thigh up into and between mine. Caresses turned into gropes and white knuckles clenched white sheets. Her sweat dripped down onto me. Moans sank into sighs and the whispered come-ons took over the room. We pulled into one another until my skin was hers and hers was mine and I could taste her fantasies before they were voiced and she showed me mine before I could think. I felt her hot breath on my skin.

Then. There was simply an arm around my waist. She had laid an arm around my waist and pulled me in close. Whispered my name into a spot just below my ear and ran her hands down my arms when I shivered from the sound.

I debated staying over and probably should have. But it meant that I would have had to stop at the Gap in the morning and buy work clothes and I didn't know what time they opened. I couldn't look at her on the way out and stumbled past her to the cab waiting outside.

I had a hard time processing it all. Figuring out where I was and who I thought I might be. My past, present and future tense were tangled up and didn't agree with one another. I was the good girl. The girl who didn't. I was the girl who told Todd Miller that Satan was in a Blondie album. I wanted to burn AC/DC's *Back in Black* so they wouldn't darken my soul. I was saved twice by Southern Baptist preachers at tent revivals. I had wanted Jesus in my heart so badly it made me cry for the relief of salvation forever and ever Amen. The promise of cotton candy, but also because I wanted Jesus in my heart.

I had believed in it all. Every bit of it. I had made out with boys in the back of the Sonic and in the dark corners of the city cemetery. I had driven down to the lake with boys and let them get just so far, because I liked to kiss more than anything else. I liked to kiss long and hard and hot. And I'd find whoever I could to kiss me. And I didn't know where it had happened. Couldn't find the point along the way that I became a girl who packed her toothbrush in anticipation of a night with another girl. A girl who walked home after dates with her lips swollen red. I didn't understand it and I wondered if I might be going to hell. I wondered. But what I knew for sure was that I still liked to kiss. I still liked it long and hard and hot and I liked it even more when I knew I could reach under her shirt and feel her nipples growing hard under my touch. I liked how I flushed when she told me I was beautiful and I knew then. I knew for sure. That if I were going to hell, I was putting on the Blondie CD. And turning it up as loud as it would go.

There were two messages waiting for me when I got back from Roxanne's. They were both from Kim. I put off calling her back. I wasn't sure what to say. When I finally picked up the phone, she told me her grandfather was in the hospital. She told me she'd been trying to get through to me for hours. She asked me if I had been with someone else.

I had been caught and I didn't want to admit it. I started crying and said, "I thought you said we could see other people."

There was silence. I didn't know what else to say and I could hear her catch her breath.

"I didn't think we could *sleep* with other people."

Kim had been making plans to come to New York to visit. I had agreed to pay half the ticket and we seemed to spend most of the phone call dealing with the financial logistics of that plane ticket. I thought she might still come to visit me. I couldn't understand why she said she didn't want to see me. I kept trying to avoid the fact that I had slept with someone else.

I had wanted someone to touch me and tell me I was sexy. I wanted to be needed and to be held. The phone calls and brief trips between Minnesota and New York hadn't been doing it and I didn't have the words to tell her. I wasn't ready to be "the bad one" yet. I wasn't ready to accept that I had hurt Kim's feelings. I didn't want to admit that I had done anything wrong. So I didn't accept anything. Instead, I talked about how to pay off the plane ticket.

When I got off the phone, I started cleaning my baseboards. I couldn't get the dirt out of the corners. I didn't want to see dust on the white paint. I wanted the corners of my rooms to sparkle. I didn't want to have to think about any of it, so I pulled out the bucket.

My mother came to visit. She was in town for the tall ships that were making their way through New York Harbor over that Fourth of July holiday. My mother had a fascination with oceans and ships and waves. She had never lived on the water in her life. I didn't know if she was coming to see me or the tall ships.

The same weekend, Rachel decided she needed to get rid of her entertainment unit. Being the proud owner of virtually no furniture, and desperately needing a good excuse to leave my apartment, my mother and my memories of what I had done to Kim, I decided to take it off her hands. I made arrangements with my landlord's furniture company to pick the piece up at Rachel's Park Slope apartment and bring it the 20 miles across Brooklyn to my place in Midwood. The entire process had to be done on a Sunday as one of the movers was Orthodox. While I was at Rachel's waiting for the movers to show up, I called my mom to see what she was up to at my apartment. I wondered if she was going through my books and reading the dog-eared passages. She sounded excited when she picked up the phone.

"You'll never believe it. I've been cleaning your apartment all day. You'll die when you see it. Your blinds were filthy and your base-boards were filthy!"

I told her the deli meat was in the crisper and I hung up.

Nothing was ever clean enough for my mother, a fact I'm sure she would dispute. She could point out the lint on top of the refrigerator. She'd tell you she couldn't care less about what was and what wasn't dirty. She would explain the base of the toilet and the grime it collects.

My mom had a lot of unspoken rules around the idea of cleaning. We cleaned the house top to bottom on Thursday nights. She would always say, "You know you won't want to do it on Friday, you'll want to do something else on Saturday and Sunday's church." We never questioned any of it.

We never questioned her about a lot of things. My mother never talked to my sister or me about sex. I learned about it with Deirdre Clark, which isn't the way it sounds. Deirdre was my best friend and her mother was what the rest of the town considered to be "a little loose" because she was divorced. We would go to the Piggly Wiggly with her mom on Saturday mornings to do the groceries and we'd ask her questions while we walked the aisles. I remember Deirdre asking how big a penis was, only I think she used the word "dick," which was scandalous in its brazenness and right there in the store, too. Deirdre's mom picked up a ketchup bottle and said, "Right about like this." We were suitably shocked and looked down at ourselves like we could see into our clothes and determine how something like that was supposed to go into us.

These kinds of questions were off-limits to my mom. My mom was good and right and went to church every Sunday and had never been divorced.

This was the first time my mother had ever seen my apartment in Brooklyn. She had visited twice when I was married and living in Manhattan. It took her over a year to come see me after I left the marriage. I think she had been as shocked as I was that the marriage had ended so abruptly. We rarely talked about it and whenever she tried to broach the subject, I would cut her short with silence. My mother blamed herself that I had gotten married. She thought she should have stopped it. She would tell me stories about how miserable I was the day I picked out my wedding dress. She thought she could have prevented the marriage, the yelling, the moving to Brooklyn, if she had just thought to refuse to buy me the dress.

I let her believe it.

In the months after I left, she would apologize and I would refuse to acknowledge her pain, because I wanted someone else to be responsible. I wanted someone else to hurt. I didn't want to admit that I had loved myself so little I had chosen to live with someone who hit me.

My mother kept asking me why I had moved to Brooklyn instead of back to Nashville "where I belonged." I didn't know how to answer that question so I told her I loved New York. I didn't know how to explain that I needed to see if I could do it on my own. I didn't know how to tell her that he had told me so many times that I would fuck up on my own, that I had to make sure he wasn't right. I didn't have the words to explain that I was afraid he might be right, so I had to prove him wrong.

My mother had moved six hours away, by car, from her mother. I was two hours away by plane. We tried to connect with one another beyond comments on our cleaning abilities. I knew that she loved me, but I wanted solid proof that she was proud of me. I wanted her to tell me that she understood me, or at least that she wanted to try. I never gave her the opportunity to do it, though. I didn't understand enough of myself to be able to share any of my life with her. My mother had always been so strong and so fierce. She had kept my family together when the world and my father's periodic unemployment and the general stress of never having enough money had tried to rip us apart. I had believed in my mother. She had kept me safe. Yelled at teachers and school administrators for me. Taught me how to get a job and make money. Showed me how to maneuver in the world. I had never seen my mother cry. I never wanted to tell her how much I hurt. How those years in that marriage had made me small and bruised and bloodied. I didn't want her to know that her little girl hurt so much. So I kept silent. I told her the baseboards looked great.

With strict Orthodox rules between the genders, the guy moving my entertainment center from Rachel's apartment wasn't allowed to shake my hand and looked pained when his assistant wanted me to sit between them on the ride back to my apartment. Having lived for over a year surrounded by Orthodox Jewish rules, I had to explain the drill before he'd slide over. The assistant was Finnish and had come to the United States the month before. He went into great detail about the differences between the countries, but his entire theory seemed to rest on the idea that, "Finnish girls when they're babies, their first word is mama. American girls first word is money."

I decided not to question him and instead deducted the comment from the tip I had planned to give them both.

By the end of her visit, my jaw was tight from the things I didn't allow myself to say to my mother. I was tired of it. I was tired of the tears burning behind my eyes and my blood pressure rising. On the way out the door my mother said, "So I'll see you probably next at Christmas?"

"Maybe," I said.

"I'll send you a ticket."

"I'll see."

I knew I was supposed to be a better person. I realized that. At the ideal Hallmark level I was supposed to love my mom into being my best friend and tell her everything. I wasn't strong enough to do it. I couldn't handle her pain when I hadn't fixed my own.

I let her walk away.

I was angry with myself for refusing to tell my mother about my pain. I looked at my grandmother's quilt hanging on my wall. I understood the anger. The rage. The black hell that could boil up in you after you'd been busted in the mouth again and you decided that time. That one time. You weren't going to *fucking* take it any more. I knew. I knew why my mothers stood proud.

I knew why their backs were of steel and their lips were all thin pressed. They were not bitter or hard, as grainy black and white photographs of them standing tall on wedding days, standing silently by new cars, or just standing quietly by their men would have you believe. They did not live to sit around a front porch to spin you stories over shelled peas. At night their hands ached from too many dishes washed and not nearly enough caresses felt.

I knew why my mothers stood proud. I knew how they scrimped on too little income and too much out-go to arrange for Christmas presents. I knew how they juggled the checkbook the creditors and the United States Postal Service in order to get the bills paid marginally on time and have enough left over for a once-a-month dinner out at McDonald's. I knew.

I knew why my mothers stood proud while their men drank and cussed and generally shook their fists at the sky in a futile attempt to make all that glitters theirs. And rather than shake their fists, my mothers shook their heads and went about the day-to-day business of living. Counters to be wiped down, meals to be fixed, children to be watched over.

I knew. I understood why my mothers stood proud while the world swirled around in a force that did not, does not, and will not include them in its marketing schemes. Upper class, middle class, buying class, does not, will not and has not included the cracker class. Their dresses were homemade, their jobs were beneath their minds and their souls were spit upon by the daily injustices that accumulated without others even seeing them. My mothers were invisible.

I knew why my mothers stood proud, stood their ground and stood in one spot. They knew what grounded them. Kept the world of too many mortgages, creditors and hungry mouths to feed from knocking them over. I was not better because I took a step outside. I was one of them. And I understood. I knew why my mothers my aunts my grandmothers my cousins my sisters my second cousins-in-law twice removed continued to stand proud. I knew while sitting in my Brooklyn apartment, staring at my borrowed furniture and my grandmother's quilt on a stark, barren wall. I knew going into my cubicle in the tall, steel building in midtown Manhattan. I knew my mothers stood proud. Because the alternative was to allow the world to knock you over.

9

I GREW up on Horace Barnes Road. The post office designated it Route 2. There were only two routes served by our post office. Sometime while I was in college, the 911 faction came through and gave us a house number. I have no idea what it was. I rarely mailed things back home, and when I did, I'd put, "Route 2, Box 133" and it would get there.

I remember trying to order Sea Monkeys out of the back of a *Richie Rich* comic book. The order blank asked for a Rural Route number. What did they mean by rural? I had a route number. But there were houses on our road other than ours. I couldn't imagine that we would be considered rural.

From 1978 to 1989, the county school district sent Lydia in Bus #4 to pick us up. Every day from late August to early May, Lydia took us to the elementary school, seven miles to the east. When we were the appropriate age, we switched to bus #52 with a driver named Linda who had frosted hair and a son in my class. She took us 20 miles south to the county high school.

As soon as I could, I wheeled a 1982 Mercury Lynx out of my parents. The Lynx had been through Hurricane Hugo and refused to start in the rain. It was purchased from a fellow who had a load of cars in front of his doublewide and called the whole thing, rather optimistically, *Bluegrass Auto Sales*. For my junior and senior years of high school, I skipped the bus routes and drove that '82 Lynx down Highways 62 and 95 and over to the high school myself.

Sometimes when I'm commuting on the Q train over the Manhattan Bridge and into Manhattan itself. I let go of the hand rails and see if I can keep my balance. Feel the rhythm of the train.

We used to do that in the back of Bus #4 going down narrow, one-lane Horace Barnes Road. Stand in the aisles and bus surf. Going around 90-degree corners that skirted the edges of McKim's Orchard, which hadn't been an orchard as long as I could remember.

I try to hold Bus #4 on Rural Route #2 and the Q Train on the Manhattan Bridge in my head at one time. Sometimes I can manage it.

It was Tuesday and I was standing on the elevated platform of my subway station wishing I had remembered to buy batteries for my Walkman and wondering if, since I had forgotten something simple like two double-A batteries, it was possible that I had also forgotten to put on some article of clothing that my employer had deemed necessary for the act of sitting in a cubicle. As it was Tuesday and not the more casual Friday, there were many dress code guide-lines to be checked. In the process of running through the list, I failed to note the woman standing beside me until we had both pushed our way onto the Q train.

Apparently not beholden to any set of dress codes, this woman was a walking, talking collection of the brightest plaids and florals to be found in the Salvation Army's back-of-the-store dollar bins. She was navigating morning rush with her very own metallic blue shop-ping cart. She was every non-pinstriped fantasy that the rest of us worker bees on the morning express could conjure up on a day when the in-box reached too high and the out-box was situated too far away to do any good. We dreamed of freedom on those days we spent enclosed in the fabric-covered walls of our cubicles, when what we really wanted to be doing was running through whatever fields of our imagination remained, or at least searching for a really good sale at the Nine West outlet down the street. Anything other than making our Monday through Friday drudge into the heart of the city armed only with a lukewarm container of coffee that was likely to spill.

This woman mocked us with her devil-may-care grin and hundreds of glittering butterfly clips covering her amber waves of hair. She sneered at our morning commuter ways of sitting quietly in the seats provided to us by the Metropolitan Transit Authority and she refused to play in any of our reindeer games by reading the *Daily News, New York Post* or the optional foreign-language weekly. She abstained from the morning rituals, stepped back from the pre-approved conventions and struck out on her own. Once we were on the train, she extracted from the cluttered depths of her metallic blue shopping cart a system of bent aluminum and cloth which, when fashioned under her watchful gaze, became her own seat. It was genius.

We shuffled our feet and our corporate-approved black messenger bags nervously when her fingers edged once again toward the inner recesses of that metallic blue shopping cart. The act of bringing her own seat had disrupted the state of affairs on the Q train quite enough. Our eyes had been opened to ways that were not our own and inner cubicle walls were crashing down all around when the *Woman of a Thousand Butterfly Clips* took us one step further. She calmly reached into her cart and pulled out a large Tupperware bowl. Eyebrows were raised up and down the subway car, anxious to see what the bowl contained, and we were not to be disappointed. Not content with the bagel and coffee of our world, this *Woman of a Thousand Butterfly Clips* had struck a blow for simplicity and convenience by packing a bowl of banana pudding.

My morning commutes set the tone for the entire day, and one morning I heard a country song playing on the radio. I stood on the concrete median while waiting for my bus, in the middle of Kings Highway. Cars and delivery vans rushed past. A pile of Puerto Rican kids jostled their way to the front of the bus line and I turned up the music with a twang going into my earphones. My toe started tapping and all I wanted to do was to put on my long, green, gingham checked sundress and dance around in a wheat field. Or find a pick-up truck and someone who made me felt as hot as a Southern Sunday and head off down to the lake for some serious relationship building.

The song playing was about working men and women. How we're all one. How we're all in it together. And I was feeling all cocky. All one with my people. I was feeling blue collar and proud and, "Pass that girl a Bud already 'cause the cooler is packed honey."

I twirled around a bit with the song and my people and steel workers and, "Aren't we all one big hard-working, flag-waving, money-saving family?" I stopped at McDonald's on the way in to work for my regular sausage n' egg biscuit. Smiled at the security guards, got that warm glow of, "Aren't I someone?" when the head of communications threw a "good morning" at me. And the first person I saw in the break room was Elizabeth. Elizabeth was our floor's mail person. Each floor had a mail person to fill our in-boxes and take our out-boxes.

Elizabeth used to call me her homey. I thought that made me cool and I loved her for it. We used to joke and do a whole Brooklyn versus the Bronx thing. Whenever the cubicle culture got to be too much for me on the 34th floor, I would sneak down into the mail-room to shoot the breeze with Elizabeth.

I walked into the break room with my McDonald's bag and my "one with the people" country anthem flowing through my head and I started ribbing Elizabeth about why she was getting a bag of bar-b-que chips and a Pepsi for breakfast. She looked right at me. She looked right at me in my Gap khakis and my Nine West shoes. She looked at me in my $50 haircut and my $27 lipstick. She looked at me with my recently-acquired middle class accessories and said,

"I eat what I can afford and I can't afford McDonald's."

I looked down at my shoes and walked away. I felt like every asshole in the world who had made me feel poor for the wrong clothes, the wrong shoes, the wrong teeth, the wrong goddamned breakfast.

I remembered what it was like to dig in the cushions of the couch to find your lunch money. I remembered clothes from the Salvation Army, the Goodwill, the yard sale on the corner because that's all there was. I remembered when a dinner out at McDonald's was a treat. I did. I did know.

But I couldn't stand there in my Gap khakis and tell Elizabeth from the Bronx and most recently of the mailroom that I got it. That I understood. Because maybe I didn't. Maybe I didn't get it anymore. Maybe I never really did. Maybe it was all faint memories and cute stories about *Folks Back Home* and *When I Was Growin' Up* and daddy and mamma and we were poor but we had love. Throw in a few cricks and hollers and country roads, just for good measure and subtle effect mind you. Because maybe I had turned my life into a rags-to-riches tale complete with matching handbag, Nine West shoes and an *Alabama* soundtrack.

I still talked to Kim on the phone, but the visits were growing further apart and she was up in the air about whether she wanted to move to Brooklyn. I started every day by taking Tylenol Extra Strength along with a large coffee. I told myself I had to get out of the apartment once a week. I needed to develop a life in Brooklyn instead of having my heart in another time zone. I decided to drop into a movie night at the lesbian center in Park Slope.

I got myself all worked up. I kept telling myself, "I can do this. I can get a life. I can learn how to be a real lesbian. I can do this casually and no one will know." I walked around the block three times and saw two 20-year-old girls in jeans walk in. I stared down at the five-page-dress-code-approved outfit I had worn to work. I felt old and sweaty. I kept walking. I went home and hid under the covers.

I went down to the Gershwin Hotel to meet Roxanne. She wanted to celebrate finishing her master's and I wanted to make sure she hadn't forgotten about me. The Gerswhin was dark and trendy. There was a small stage where they allowed comics an almost-open-mic on certain nights. We ended up in the first row. Three comics in, and the show starts failing. The material was falling short so the comedian turned his set on us.

"So are you two lesbians or what?"

Insert the standard crowd silence here as everyone in the room turned to stare at the two dykes front and center.

Part of me was excited that I had somehow stepped out of my dress code and been seen for who I was. Who I was becoming. My inner baby rainbow started singing, "Woohoo! Everybody knows I'm a dyke!" My inner New York City bitch took over and snapped, "Goddamnit. I've got to leave here tonight and get on a subway alone with a roomful of straight people who may or may not appreciate the non-straight factor and who may or may not be so loaded up on alcohol that they take it out on me." ACT UP or not, it was damn uncomfortable.

I had gotten through most of my life by keeping my mouth shut. I stared at the stage. Roxanne shot back, "yeah" and took a drink.

He was on a roll. "So are you together or what?"

I kept my mouth shut again. Not out of an effort to look smooth, but because it was a question I had been wondering about myself. I looked at Roxanne, who took another drink.

"We're together here tonight, yeah."

The comic moved on and I got up to go to the bathroom. I still didn't understand what her answer meant.

We went out to dinner the next night to have the "where are we with this relationship" conversation. I kept my mouth shut through most of it. I didn't want those unexpected nights at her apartment to end. I had spent months looking for a definition of me. On those nights in her apartment, I found myself in a space where tangible definitions were unnecessary and dress codes irrelevant. I forgot to try so hard. She asked what my expectations were.

"I gave up having expectations."

She countered my ability to coin non-committal, corporate-like answers.

"I don't have intense feelings for you one way or the other."

I finished my tea and went home. I wished she hadn't said that. I thought we had been having a good time. I didn't want to be told that someone didn't have intense feelings one way or another.

I took out an ad on *Match.com*. I had no idea what that meant or what it was I thought I'd find there. I just generally believed in the power of the Internet to fix my life. To make it make sense again. I kept flipping through the ads online and they seemed so defined and so narrow and so little. Every lesbian in the metro area seemed to feel the need to state preferences for butch or femme. No one wanted bi's. Everyone expressed a great love for hiking, camping or the great outdoors in general. I didn't understand any of it. I liked butch and femme. I thought I might be bi, but I'd never admit it. I knew that I hated hiking, camping and the great outdoors. This was New York. I wanted someone who loved sidewalks and subways.

I asked Rachel to help me write an ad. We brainstormed. We wrote it out on napkins at the bar. I was a contradiction of terms that seemed difficult to gather into an online ad. I was the literate Southerner, the dyke who coveted her neighbor's eyeliner and my CD changer held *Loretta Lynn's Greatest Hits*, Ben Harper and The Magnetic Fields' *69 Love Songs*. I hated shopping but loved my khakis and oxford shirts. I was the corporate girl with a year's supply of body glitter.

Our attempts at ads with 60 characters or less all kept coming out, "Fun dyke iso smooching, no hikers!"

I kept answering ads on *Match.com*, trying to construct a relationship out of email. I wrote love letters to no one in an attempt to define exactly what it was I thought love might be. I sat for hours in the dark of my apartment with the sweet Southern drawl of a song drifting over me. I lit candles and let the light summer breezes drift in off the ocean. I traced the outline of my jaw from ear to chin and around my lips. I tried to remember what love had felt like. I closed my eyes and remembered Laura's blue wool coat. Its roughness scratching my cheek. How I pressed into her when she held me. I flushed from the bottoms of my soles to the back of my neck. I opened my eyes and it grew cold in July. I went back to answering emails.

I met four girls through *Match.com* that summer. I met them all at the Astor Lounge on the edge of the Lower East Side. I'd sit outside under an umbrella and I always ordered the mixed green salad with vinaigrette and drink a gin and tonic. I imagined that's what a person like me would do. I would attempt to define myself with each of those women as a model. I had stepped away from my husband, my apartment and my codified life. I had walked away from my religion, my sexuality and my culture. My cookbooks required ingredients that I couldn't find in my Brooklyn neighborhood. I would listen to these women speak of themselves in no uncertain terms and with a great degree of confidence. They knew who they were. I wanted to know, too. I spoke a lot about myself, but with a very vague and general vocabulary. I left myself open for interpretation because I wasn't sure of anything.

In my stories over gin and tonics, the blue collar became slightly denim and the *Lifetime Movie-of-the-Week* that was my marriage was filtered through a half-hour sitcom. I joked a lot about my cubicle. I wondered how much I could sublimate myself before I disappeared. I wondered how much I could speak before I scared everyone away.

I had been going to the Brooklyn Meeting of Quakers for awhile. Sometimes I dropped into their Quaker questions class afterwards. There was a long discussion one day about how one woman decided she could be both Quaker and Jewish. I had been asking myself for some time who I was, and I wanted to know how this woman had figured out who she was. I sat silently and I wondered. If I were a dyke, how could I be wearing lipstick? How could I have been married to a man? How could I be a member of the Green Party and work for a Fortune 500 company? I wanted to know how this woman had come to know who she was, because I wanted to know too.

I looked at this woman in my Quaker class and I wondered if I wore lipstick and flippy skirts because that's just who I was. I was Southern. I was raised on a steady diet of hairspray. I wanted to stop denying parts of myself and this seemed a good place to start. Being Southern and Northern, a dyke and a femme, corporate and liberal and it all meant that I got to be me. All those sappy, insipid articles I used to pore over in *Seventeen* had it right when they advised young girls to be themselves. Just. Be yourself.

I was trying. Hard. To move on. Sunday afternoon I made the mistake of actually watching the Lifetime Channel and the movie of my life was on. One of those abused woman gets the strength to leave her marriage kind of movies.

I thought I could do it. I thought I had healed so much, become so fully me that I could tune this in like every other person in America who seems quite capable of watching a woman getting hit without flinching. I thought I could watch this movie on Lifetime while reading the *New York Times* or talking on the phone or whatever it is that people do when watching a movie of the week about self-esteem shattered and options closed off.

I was doing fine. I was. I saw him hit her and I did my little reflex of "It never looks like that. It's never that dramatic."

Which is how I deal. Usually. But the Post-Traumatic Reality kicked into high gear when the movie husband yelled. The husband yelled at her about the checks being out of sequence.

The checks out of sequence.

Your honor. I confess. I confess to you, almighty Father and gathered guests that I too have sinned. It's been too long since my last confession. And I have sinned. I have written checks out of sequence.

God help me, the only phrase I was capable of summoning in my mind was,

I've been guilty of that.

I've been guilty. I've been guilty of writing checks out of sequence. Because it's still a crime in my reality. In my Post-Traumatic Reality, writing a check out of sequence is still a crime and I have paid. Oh, how I have paid. Over and over and over to make the point clear. Because this is the only way to get it through my thick, stupid skull he explains. And the tears start and they do not stop and he tells me to pull it together already, it's for my own good. This lesson, it's the only way I'll learn. I bang my head against the wall to make it stop. Make it all stop.

It does stop. Comes to a crashing halt when he yanks my hair so hard that I tumble backward out of the bed and onto the floor and Jesus Christ can't the neighbors hear this? Is 911 working anywhere in the city tonight? Because the phone is too far. And my hair is pulled and I crawl crying to the kitchen and grab a steak knife and wave it around to make it stop, make it all stop, just Jesus Christ. Make it. Make it stop.

I saw a movie of my life this weekend. I saw myself standing at the open window of a Brooklyn summer and I cried. For all that I have paid to get here. I cried for all that any woman has had to pay to enjoy a summer breeze.

 chapter

10

IT WAS earnings day at Mega Mega Corp., which meant everyone in the corporate communications department was insane. I got the press release up on the Web site and sat back to relax. I was downing my second cup of coffee when a coworker wandered by and asked, "Um, are you going to do the newsletter?"

I had forgotten. The newsletter on earnings day was easily a four-hour process that involved pissing off any number of people by hogging the copy machine for 500 seven-page copies; two trips down to the basement mailroom; and two emails to head people because I always screwed up the first one.

The department head came by in the middle of all of that and asked me if I had the budget figures for the coming year. I tore up pink FedEx slips to keep from yelling at her. I counted to ten and had a conversation with her, which was conducted entirely in my own mind. I said,

Hi Linda. See all the empty cubes? Those are people who were responsible for budget figures. I am not responsible for budget figures. Next office, please.

When I finished counting, I looked up at her with my FedEx bits surrounding me and said, "I don't have them."

She told me to tell my supervisor to get the budget figures to her by the end of the day. She hated him as much as I did. He didn't yell at her, though. He took his corporate rage out on me. I left a Post-It note on his computer telling him to do his budget numbers ASAP. I used the phrase, "per Linda" because I had a bit of corporate rage of my own and I wanted to scare him.

When he got back from lunch he called me into his office and sat me down. He looked me in the eye and said, "So, what we're going to do is to put you in charge of the budget process for the department."

He had won. I came out of the meeting and put a note about the discussion in my green hanging file folder labeled *Things To Discuss In Great Detail At Review Time*. The discussion had warranted its own manila folder which I labeled *Pissed Off*. I took the rest of the day to update my resume.

My favorite line said,

"Maintain editorial control over content, design, production and distribution of 7,500-circulation employee newsletter. Write, research, copyedit and obtain source approvals for employee magazine distributed to 75,000 employees world-wide and a professional journal circulated to 30,000 external clients. Supervise team of outside graphic designers and distributors for department publications."

I liked that it was entirely true, and yet what I mostly did was sit in my cubicle and go out to lunch on my company credit card.

On rare occasions, working with the corporate brass provided me with perks not normally afforded to those in the cubicle ranks. Linda, the head of our department, had gotten a free dinner to a fancy restaurant from one of our vendors. She decided to pass it on to the people in the department. I looked forward to it for weeks and it didn't disappoint. The dinner itself lasted three hours. The restaurant was uptown and I didn't know that places like that existed. There was dark wood paneling and waiters who were just right there with new silver, with Pellegrino, with wine, with jokes. We had pasta and antipasta. I ordered the sea bass and we drank three bottles of red wine and topped it all off with a bottle of Moet for the table. It was how New York looked in the movies. I wanted to sit in it forever. For good measure, I ran into Elizabeth Hurley on my way to the ladies room. I had to tell her, "excuse me" because I had accidentally hit her with my $10 backpack from Kmart.

I didn't know what to do with the rage left over from my marriage. I wondered how people did it. Got up in the morning, went to work and came home. Got through life without any element of the drama I was experiencing. I didn't know how to calm down. I wasn't quite sure how to *Just Be*. I stayed up until 2 a.m. cleaning the window blinds. I would consider the baseboards and wonder how best to clean them, as well. What bucket to use. What kind of cleaning solution to fill it with. If a sponge or a rag would do better. Or maybe there was an old toothbrush to get into those dark corners.

I would clean and try to remember a touch of love from him. Try to remember if there had been some kind of caress. But all I could remember were grips. Sweaty grips and heated words. Bruises discovered in showers. He told me that he loved me. He cared about me. He wanted to be near me all the time. He would worry when I was working late and he would tell me constantly that he needed me. He told me all these things, but I couldn't call up one image, one memory, a single time that he had touched me tenderly. Maybe he had. Surely he had. But all I could remember was sitting in a walk-in closet waving a wire hanger to keep him away.

The self-hatred was more than I could stand. I wanted to cry long and hard and deep and dark but I couldn't. I couldn't let myself get to that point. I wanted someone to hear the tears and understand what the hell they meant. I wanted to throw something against some wall somewhere and have it stick. The divorce hadn't gone through yet and I was still lugging around his last name. I was, according to the laws of the state, a married woman. I wanted someone to hear my pain. I wanted someone to finally hear how much it had hurt and how much it continued to hurt.

People would ask me. People always asked me, "Aren't you glad? Aren't you glad you didn't pick up those razors? Aren't you glad you made it through? Aren't you glad it's over?"

I wanted to scream.

"No. No I'm not glad. No I'll never be glad. I'm not glad that I got that close to that dark edge of nothingness. No, no I'm not glad for having seen that pit up close and personal."

No one knew how to handle my rage. Well meaning friends would pour me a drink and try to get an ounce of gratitude out of me. "Well, aren't you glad that you know who you are? Glad of where you are? Glad that you got to New York at least because you were married? Aren't you at least glad of that?"

I tried to halt the assumptions. I wanted everyone to stop assuming that I wouldn't have ended up in a midtown Manhattan skyscraper or a celebrity-filled restaurant on my own and without him. To stop assuming that it took being married to get a decent job. To stop assuming that it took being hit to truly appreciate happiness.

Because the truth of the matter was that I hadn't done all that *because* of him. I hadn't become all that I had become *because* I had been married. I had done every bit of it *in spite* of him. I had found my life, my happiness, myself, *in spite* of being hit. I moved to New York without having been farther north than Cincinnati. I had figured out how to get a Manhattan apartment in a good neighborhood without the financial backing, support, or savvy of anyone else. I had maneuvered my way up a career path and into a nice corporate cubicle with only a Kentucky regional college education.

I wanted the world to stop assuming that I had done all of this *because* I was married and he was the one who happened to get the big-time job in New York City that transferred us there.

I had a constant headache and I couldn't get my front door to lock. The August humidity had warped it so the latch wouldn't hold. I was turning into a slob. I found myself looking at little spots of dried cat upchuck and figuring I'd clean it up later. In the kitchen, coffee from a week ago was still on the counter. In the living room, two glasses tipped over so the cat could drink seltzer, too. There were dirty clothes strewn all over the place.

I told myself I had to get it together. I had begun emailing Kim again, trying to process the end of our relationship. I had been emailing girls from *Match.com* trying to begin a relationship. I had been emailing Roxanne trying to get her to feel intensely about me. I was beginning to doubt the power of the Internet in getting any of this settled satisfactorily.

Roxanne came over to my apartment for the first time. She stayed for 28 straight hours. She stayed in my bedroom. She pulled me in to my own room. She kept asking what I wanted. All I could manage was a moan and to slide my wetness down her thigh. I didn't want to tell her. I didn't want to say a thing. I didn't want her to know what I wanted because I wanted it all. I wanted her rawness and her power and her experience. I wanted every bit of her imagination to come full force down onto me.

I kept silent through the hands and fingers and thighs. Wet. She said, "Can you take this? Can you feel this? Do you want this?"

I wanted it and more. I wanted more than she could give. I said, "Yes." I said, "Yes I can. Yes I can take this. I can feel this. I want this. This right here, this wall, this bed, this couch, the floor, your hand, your leg, your entire body. I do. I do want."

I wanted it all.

I sat in my cube the next morning and stared at the walls. I tried desperately to reign it all back in. Get it back under control. I couldn't, so I left in the middle of the day. I climbed out of the midtown

Manhattan skyscraper and sunk into the depths of the Q train. I clutched my bag and refused to turn on my Walkman or open a book because I was trying. Trying to get control of my head.

The weekend was pushing its way into my Monday and it made my neck flush. In the middle of the weekend she had whispered to me, "You're scared."

I kept my mouth shut because she had been right. I had been scared. Scared that she was done with me and would go away.

I sent her an email to tell her I had a good time. To tell her I wanted more good times. To tell her I was feeling intensely about her. It had been 36 hours since the 28 hours ended and 24 hours since I hit "send" on the email. And I had heard nothing.

I had told her in an email that I wanted it all, and I knew, now, with her silence, that it wasn't going to happen.

I began to have dreams about my ex-husband. I dreamed of his dying in plane crashes and my being federally responsible for the body. I dreamed that he was about to get married again I tried to warn the new girl about him. In the middle of trying to warn her, I realized I didn't have to warn her, because he didn't hit her. He had just hit me. I was the one who got hit, because I was the one who had deserved it.

I no longer knew what to think, or what to expect. I didn't have any idea what I deserved. I wanted someone to look at me and see me. Just me. A girl sitting in a cubicle. I wanted someone to look at me and understand that I loved my commutes, desired a good donut and an even better coffee. I wanted someone to get why it was that I loved my sister and why I lived where I did. I wanted someone to laugh at my jokes and understand my obsession with baseboards. I wanted to show someone the books I kept under my bed without fear that they would think less of me. I wanted to carry my Emma Goldman into the corporate cafeteria without concealing the cover. I wanted a nice green salad with a vinaigrette dressing for dinner and a better CD collection than I could afford. I wanted Roxanne to call. I wanted someone to hold me in the night. I wanted to know that I wasn't the only one to get hit. I wanted to know that I hadn't deserved it after all.

Roxanne had not contacted me. There had been one phone call and two emails, all of which had gone unanswered.

I had a list of things I did when I was depressed. I would check them off one by one until I hit on something that worked. Sometimes my ex-therapist's mantra reverberated in my head until I thought the pounding it caused would drive me insane. "You gain self-esteem by doing esteem-able acts!"

I had no idea what she meant by that. I stuck to my list. I put on *ABBA*. I showered under the disco ball and forced myself to stare at its reflection and contemplate its beauty. I drank a lot of coffee and told coworkers we should all ditch casual Fridays and have the city institute a policy of "Disco Fridays" instead. I wanted everyone to be in gold lamè. In the middle of my list, I received an email from Roxanne informing me that she had no intense feelings for me, which is why she hadn't called back after our long weekend together. She wrote that she was incredibly sure that we would never be more. She wrote,

Despite hanging out with you for a full day to try to convince myself to the contrary, I still just like you a lot.

I went into the bathroom and cried. The department head called and told us to all go home early. That it was too nice a day to be working. I walked downstairs and into the subway. I needed to get off the grid. The streets in Manhattan — those above 14th Street — are laid out on a grid. They make sense. The streets below 14th Street are a mishmash. There's no way to make your way around unless you know exactly where you're going and you've been there before. I need-ed to get downtown. I needed to get lost. I got on the Q train and went to Grand Street in the heart of Chinatown.

You get the full effect of Chinatown only if you walk slowly, so I did. I stared at live eels for sale. I was pushed aside by people selling pirated CDs and DVDs. I heard voices that made no sense to me. I wandered through aquarium stores and stared at the large Oranda goldfish. I made my way to Bluestockings. I was the only one there in a suit and I tried to hide. I sat in a corner and I pulled out some poetry books. No one could see me and I read. I had reached the end of my list. And at the bottom of it was "New York City." That was the thing about New York. It was always there. I felt the blood rush back into my toes and I stopped feeling dizzy. I gathered up my things and went home.

I wanted to be mysterious and unapproachable. I wanted to be unflappable. I wanted piercings and red dyed hair. I wanted the humidity to go away. I wanted more sleep and a Burger King that delivered. Instead, I sat in a cubicle decked out in corporate-approved clothing. I wrote memos and newsletters that no one read and I talked to my mail person because no one else would listen. I drank coffee and I stayed on my game so I would at least look self-assured. For days, I stared at the email Roxanne had sent me.

I still just like you a lot.

What was so insane. What bothered me the most. Was that I just liked her too.

But she said it first.

I made plans to go to dinner and a movie with another girl from *Match.com*. I figured she would probably try to convince herself to the contrary and realize that she really just liked me, too. We went out for Malaysian food and I sat across the table at dinner trying to let her know how fabulous I was. Unfortunately, what I really did was talk about my mother a lot. The date was going poorly. I was completely mortified. I wondered if she was too. I tried being the person I was at work because I wasn't sure what else to do and I needed some confidence. I found myself saying "power structures" a lot. At some point in the evening I turned obnoxious. I completely forgot about charming. She yawned. I tried talking about poetry and got side-tracked. I lost my point. I wanted to explain how socialist I was. It went nowhere. I mentioned the movie *Footloose* three times. Kevin Bacon was mentioned twice. The word "three-wheeler" was introduced to the conversation. I went to the bathroom and tried to compose myself. It was raining and my hair looked horrible. I hadn't dressed as well as I had thought. I wanted to go home.

The second time she and I went out, I took her to the Rising for drinks. We sat in the corner. She was dressed in leather and I kept touching her arm. I made her sit with me until the bar closed. I didn't want to go home. I wanted someone to sit with me while I watched the bartender. As the night went on, the bar grew packed, the room filled with cigarette smoke and the music grew louder. The bartender had on a black tank top and black jeans. She was tall and thin and her arms were ripped. She had a large, silver rodeo buckle on her belt. She had black cowboy boots and a black hat. She slipped me drinks. At the end of the night, everyone forgot their roles. The bartender stepped out from behind the bar and started to dance. She moved her long, summer legs in those boots. Those boots that should have weighed down her being and instead just served to ground her hips. Ground her hips as she moved to the DJ's beat in a Brooklyn night. I kissed my date good-night on the corner because I no longer cared if the guys standing in front of the bodega saw me or not. She didn't seem interested in anything more, so I found separate livery cabs to take us to our own apartments.

I had a long talk with my cab driver. I hadn't spoken a complete paragraph with my date, but the cab driver seemed safe. He didn't want a relationship from me and I appreciated that. I knew I wouldn't receive emails from him telling me that despite attempts at spending time with me, he still just liked me. We talked a lot. He was from

Mexico City and he showed me pictures of his kids.

"No, no I don't have any myself," I told him. "Yours are beautiful."

He told me his ex-wife was insane. I told him we had a lot in common. He gave me a high-five. He told me I needed a boyfriend.

"I'm off that. I'm off boys; I'm having fun."

He gave me another high-five over the backseat.

He told me I needed to dance more. That I should do the merengue. That I should salsa every night after work. I laughed and leaned back in the seat. I told him I'd think about it and I tipped him $10.

I was sinking further into a depression and my list wasn't helping me. I could hear crickets outside my bedroom window. The dishes needed washing. The laundry guy rang my bell three times but I didn't feel like dealing with him so I let him leave the bag out front and told myself I'd pay him later. I got called by the Visa people. Apparently the plan to not pay bills in August failed miserably. I started to explain the humidity to her, but she was in Memphis. She stopped my babbling and said, "Listen, if you want humidity you come here. Now, when can we expect payment?"

I didn't have a good answer for her so I hung up the phone without answering.

My 29th birthday was coming up and it bothered me. I had expected to be more by the time I was 29. Rachel heard the pain in my voice and used her company's messenger service to send me a pint of Ben & Jerry's New York Super Fudge Chunk, the *Saturday Night Fever* soundtrack, a bag of Fritos and a large package of Sour Patch Kids. I still felt myself reeling.

The day before my birthday, I went into Manhattan to buy a new outfit for the party Rachel had planned for me. I walked along Lafayette Street on the south side. I saw him walking along Lafayette Street on the north side. Him, the husband. I hadn't seen him in over a year. I hadn't seen him since I kissed him good-bye on his way to

Seattle. I wondered if he still thought of himself as married or if he told people he was divorced, even though we were definitely still married. I still had his name as mine. I saw him and it scared me. I wasn't a person who was easily scared. As a child I used to run outside and chase thunderstorms. I had slept through a tree falling on my house and I once stood in front of a sliding-glass door and watched a tornado destroy a lumber mill. I had strolled down abandoned subway tracks. I had walked home drunk at 4 a.m. and stood on empty train platforms in the wee hours of the morning. I went days without locking my front door and I yelled at creditors, at bill collectors and at the guy who signed my paycheck.

I did not get scared.

I did not get scared until I started walking down Lafayette Street. I told myself that no one had ever died on Lafayette Street at noon. I thought I could walk across Lafayette and past the steel fence that went around the Catholic school. I used to stare at that fence and imagine he'd bash my head over it. I walked past the pay phone at the corner where I'd sneak out to make calls. I walked past the grocery store he'd yell at me to go to because I was so fucking stupid I'd forgotten to buy the right kind of croutons. I thought maybe I could walk down Lafayette Street without getting scared and the second I crossed the boundary of the Bowery, every nerve, every single nerve in my body was on edge and frozen. Muscles tense. Mind racing. And everyone seemed to be walking too slowly.

I saw him on the corner of the street. It was my birthday eve.

I stopped. I turned around. I slunk into the shadows of a parking lot. I wondered what he looked like. Wondered if he had changed at all. I wondered if had lost weight as a result of my not buying the correct croutons for him. I turned around and saw that he hadn't changed a bit.

The birthday itself was better than I expected. Rachel arranged for an odd assortment of friends to meet at one of our favorite bars in

Park Slope. It had an outdoor patio and we took it over en mass. She bought some plastic bubbles, poppers with streamers, and tiaras. We made friends with the table next to us. They blew bubbles with us and tried on the tiaras. We ordered pitchers of beer and there was a light summer breeze. The patio was surrounded by white, twinkly Christmas lights and Rachel gave me a Tiffany's box with a silver necklace nestled inside.

We closed the bar, then went back to her apartment and had cupcakes.

I got home and discovered that Kim had sent me an overnight package filled with CDs and videos and glitter polish for my nails. I sank into bed and tried to remember what it felt like to not go through life scared.

Roxanne and I had moved steadily into the category of "just friends" after an incredible amount of emailing and phone calling. We went out to the movies regularly and found ourselves in a bar on Second Avenue after one of them.

We walked in, ordered our drinks and got in two good sentences of conversation before we heard someone raise his voice in our direction.

"Goddamn dykes. What the fuck? Stupid dykes."

The next night, I went out again. This time with another girl. I decided I needed a change of scenery, so I took the F train instead of the D. It required a 20 block bus ride and then a climb up an elevated station. Underneath the tracks was a car service decorated with Puerto Rican flags and a second-hand furniture store that I kept thinking I should go to and never did. There was a newsstand. There always seemed to be newsstands.

I debated whether it was too late at night to chance waiting alone on the platform, or if I should bide my time below, in view of the token booth operator. I don't know what safety and protection I thought he could provide locked up behind his Plexiglas window. But it seemed a good night to be aware.

I was still feeling the effects of the "goddamn dykes" comment. I never knew who to trust. I went up to the platform rather than stand in front of the token booth clerk. I sat down on the wood bench nicely provided for me by the Metropolitan Transit Authority of New York City and pulled out my book. Nothing happened. The train came. I got on and did my thing. Nothing happened.

When I got home, I searched my cupboards for something quick to eat. I bit down on a corn pop that the CVS across the street had put into a convenient canister for my snack food needs. Something went crack. I made an appointment to see the dentist. I hadn't been in two years. She took one look and told me I had a fractured tooth. I asked how much. She picked the figure $1,200 out of the air. My insurance would pay for a chunk, but I was responsible for $480.

I thought I handled the whole thing pretty well. There had been reasons I hadn't gone to the dentist in two years. I sat in the chair and focused on breathing and trying to keep calm. I started crying in the chair. I hated having people of authority force things into my mouth and I didn't need a therapist to figure out why. I grabbed the bill, made the appointment to get the tooth fixed and went home to sleep for three hours.

I ran my budget numbers and factored in the amount I had to pay for my tooth. I was out of money. Seriously out of money. I stared at my favorite postcard, taped to the bulletin board in my cubicle. It asked me daily, "Want some happy?" I kept looking at it and whispering, "yes." I pictured myself as a grownup. Someone who went to bed on time and did yoga. I imagined that I would eat granola and wheat germ or some kind of pop-tarted form of tofu. It was a great image. It was the one in which I drank plenty of water and had accessories that accessorized and my checkbook was always perfectly balanced. In this grownup world of mine, I had a budget and made doctor's appointments and my CD collection was mostly always in order.

As it was, I never got to bed before midnight and I cursed the dawn. I never exercised and I could barely be bothered to carry an umbrella when it rained. I thought I had lost my silver thumb ring and it freaked me out. I had been playing with it at lunch and then at 2 p.m. I realized I didn't have it on and I almost started crying. I had bought that ring for myself on my birthday the year before. I had given myself some around-the-way vow about cleaving unto myself and no one else and I thought I had lost it.

It was at home under the bathroom sink.

I still didn't have the money for the dentist.

I called my mother. I wanted to ask her for money for my teeth, without really asking her. I could never tell her what I needed, which forced our conversations to take place on two levels. It was a very complicated system we had been working on for almost thirty years, wherein she said one thing and I assumed another. What follows is a transcript of me asking for money without asking for money:

"So I'm having $1,200 worth of dental work to fix an old, old filling."

Subtext: Because when I was a kid we didn't have enough money to have this done right so now my tooth is frigging fractured.

"Don't you have dental insurance?"

Subtext: How the hell do you think you can live on your own? You are so unorganized.

"I have insurance, I still have to pay $500. I'm not sure how I'm going to do it. Eat mac n' cheese for a month I guess."

Subtext: Yes mother, of course I have insurance and I am in fact somewhat organized. That said, I could use a loan.

"You need some new glasses too."

Subtext: I'm not giving you a cent. Shut up about your teeth already. If you had bought glasses when I told you to, your teeth would be fine.

"It was good to talk to you."

Subtext: No it wasn't.

End of phone call.

For comparison's sake, I also tracked my phone conversation with my laundry guy.

"Uhhhh grumble.. uhhhhh.. Hello?"

Subtext: No one ever calls but you.

"Um, yeah. Hi. I was wondering if you could pick up my laundry today?"

Subtext: Please come bring me clean socks.

"Oh! You! Sure sure sure. You live in that house on Kings Highway, right?"

Subtext: Ok.

"Thanks!"

Subtext: Thanks.

End of phone call.

It was easy to tell my laundry guy what I needed. I doubted I'd ever have the guts to tell my mother I needed her.

 chapter

11

I HAD interviewed with a company in the World Trade Center. The headhunter said they loved me. They wanted me to come back and talk to one other person. This would be the fourth interview for one job. I told her it was getting a bit much. I told her I couldn't keep taking time off work to travel downtown and talk to people who may or may not hire me. The headhunter started talking salary. She said they were talking a range that was $5,000 more than I was making at Mega Mega. I couldn't believe they were yanking me around for a barely-there increase.

"You know what, that much of an increase isn't worth the effort of planning a new commute."

The headhunter said she'd see what she could do.

"You do that," I snapped as I hung up.

The whole thing was annoying me. Mega Mega might have been boring as hell, but it was a known boring. I could handle boring. I could take a good, long, turn at boring.

The headhunter called back with an interview time that was more convenient for me and another bump in the salary. I grabbed my pen and wrote the times down in my day planner.

When I came up out of the subway in Times Square after the

fourth and final interview I saw a three-story billboard proclaiming in bright yellows and reds,

It's All About You.

Someone had finally gotten it right. The interview had gone well and I had country music playing in my Walkman. I was wearing tights and my new lipstick. I wanted that job and I had told them what they wanted to hear in order to get it.

The headhunter called and said, "You met with a lot of people and to a person, they all said they loved you. That's really unusual."

I told her, "I'm a loveable person, Joan."

I calculated the raise I would be getting. It was 20 percent over what I was making at Mega and 50 percent more than I was making just two years before. I sat in my cubicle and composed a letter to my boss.

Dear Stupid Boss Man:

I quit.

Love,

The Cubicle Girl

When I finally got up the nerve to tell my boss in a more appropriate format, with a typed resignation letter on bond paper, he asked,

"So, what? Are you unhappy here?"

I thought about all the lunch reservations he had me make for him. How often he had yelled at me for the heat not coming on in his office. The times he made it seem my fault for the magazine missing its deadline.

I wanted to say, *No, you dill weed. I love it here. I'm just a sadist in the category of work and I thought I'd screw myself over. I'll go home now and beat myself with horsehair.*

But I restrained myself, because I had gotten really good at not saying what I wanted to say. Instead, I mumbled, "This is a really good opportunity for me." And walked out.

It was a beautiful moment.

I was feeling righteous. Righteous over Mrs. Cates in the first grade who put me in the sub-par reading group despite my straight As. Over Mrs. Roberts in the second grade who sniffed every time she saw my garage sale clothes. Over all the teachers in high school who told me I should consider a community college despite my high test scores. Over assholes who had laughed at my Kentucky accent. And over my ex-husband. I wanted to yell, "Ha! The white trash wins!"

Work was important to me. I had always wanted to be rich, or at least not poor. I had always been hungry and sometimes been poor and pretty much always wanted to be rich. I had my first resume when I was 15.

"You were that accomplished at 15?" a friend asked once.

And the answer was no. I wasn't that accomplished, but I was that hungry and I never wanted to be poor. We were poor as kids. It was something we were never supposed to acknowledge. It changed over time, so we were able to forget the Christmas holidays where my dad worked overtime to get $25 for a present. We were the paycheck-to-paycheck family. The people who calculated to the minute when the mortgage check would clear the bank and then plan meals of bologna and water accordingly.

I had dug in the cushions of the couch for lunch money and picked out school clothes at garage sales and from bags of cast-offs of well-meaning church friends. I never wanted to be poor. Being poor didn't mean that you were hungry, dirty or greasy-haired. It didn't mean that you wished for a new car or wanted to go on European vacations. It didn't mean you were stupid and didn't know any better.

It meant being invisible. It meant that people made assumptions about you and passed judgments on you and you were relegated to the corners of life without your even knowing it. I wore clothes that were too tight, too small and too two-seasons-ago, so I was told to go to the back of the class. So at 15, I went to the local newspaper and presented my resume in response to an ad for a typesetter.

I sang and I danced in appropriate quantities for *The Man,* who was otherwise known as Lloyd, and who will always and forever have a soft spot in my heart. Lloyd liked what he saw on my resume and he laughed at my 15-year-old jokes. He was particularly taken with the fact that I lived around the corner from him.

My first day on the job, Lloyd came over to see how it was going. He looked at me hunting and pecking on the keyboard.

"Um. I didn't know you didn't know how to type!"

I turned around and looked at him.

"You didn't ask."

He let me keep the job.

Things were changing and it all left me feeling unsure. Mega had been the one remaining constant in my life. The black steel skyscraper in midtown had been my financial and emotional safety net when everything else in my life was falling apart. I kept staring out the windows of the company's cafeteria on the 35th floor. I would look at the World Trade Center towers on the edge of Manhattan. My new office would be there. I thought it would make my dad proud.

When we were little, we would go on drives. Anywhere we could think of to go, but mostly to Paducah. It was the biggest town near us and had both a mall and a store with an elevator. My dad liked to drive us up to the Jackson House in Paducah. It was a residential center for senior citizens and it was six stories tall. He would drive up to the front of it and say, "Look at that kids. That's Paducah's skyscraper."

I sent my dad a postcard of the New York skyline with the World Trade Center circled. On the back I wrote, "Look. That's a New York skyscraper, and where I'm going to work!"

I called my parents to tell them about the new job. I would be working closely with the CEO. He was from Europe and had a corner office. I was from Possum Trot and had a cubicle. I told my mom I was nervous. I was looking for reassurance or at least a pat on the back. I wanted her to tell me she was proud of me for having gotten from Kentucky to the World Trade Center.

"I feel nervous. I feel I like I shouldn't be talking to a CEO. I feel like I shouldn't be working in a building like the World Trade Center."

There was a silence.

"No. No, you're right. You really shouldn't."

I didn't know what to make of it. I couldn't find any pride in her statements. I turned the conversation to the weather and hung up as soon as I could.

I started to compensate for the lack of any real interpersonal connections in my life. I developed a series of complex and intense relationships with people I interacted with on a daily basis. They were mostly irrelevant relationships and yet completely necessary to my existence.

A woman at the CVS showed me a bargain on disposable razors. She told me,

"You should really start reading the circulars when you shop."

I agreed. She saved me $4, so I bought a Nutrageous bar. The McDonald's woman gave me my food before I even ordered. I got my large coffee, no sugar, no cream without a word. One Sunday the guy at the bodega asked me why I wasn't buying a *New York Times*.

I liked it when people noticed.

I would have half-hour conversations about capitalism, immigration and the fact that the beer selection was limited to Colt 45 and Bud Light with the guy who sat behind the counter at the bodega. The bagel guy would give me updates on his rather extensive plans to enroll at some community college and major in business. I found myself wandering the aisles of the CVS Pharmacy at odd hours of the night, and talking to the clerk about the powers of body glitter and how marriage was an evil visited upon the masses by God and government. She analyzed the concept of "under an hour" in terms of photo processing and I tried to remember to buy cat litter.

Those were the relationships I could handle. It was a whole different ballgame when it came to my relationship with the laundry guy.

We met thanks to the sign in his front window advertising "Free Pick Up and Delivery." Like the dutiful daughter calling home on Sunday afternoons, I did my part. I turned clean clothes into dirty ones and waited until the laundry bag was full. I would place the call for a pick-up and things would proceed steadily downhill from there.

It was a good three weeks before he was able to put address with reality and actually find the bag I left outside my door. I found myself screaming my address into the phone in some kind of misguided hope that volume alone would bridge the hick to Yemen language gap that had developed between us. It took another two months for us to get the Tuesdays- or Fridays-only pick-up schedule established. I found on occasion that I was missing socks. An entire sweater set had vanished. My towels were replaced by someone else's, and more often than not my colors bled into my whites.

I kept analyzing the situation. I wondered if I had become co-dependent. I spent entire commutes deconstructing our conversations. Wondering where I had gone wrong, if I hadn't communicated my needs properly, if I had let Laundry Guy overstep my carefully constructed boundaries. I was obsessing. I worried that I'd end my days alone in an apartment with my cat, a bag of dirty undies, and the words "laundry guy" scrawled over and over into the message pad by the answering machine. I wondered what had become of me.

I decided to change. I stopped yelling addresses into the phone and got the numbers of other laundry guys in the neighborhood. I went online and found a Laundry Guy who promised to pick up my laundry according to a schedule I chose and who would let me enter my address directly into his database. I left my name and number and the various bits of necessary information about my address. I heard a keyboard clicking in the background. It sounded so organized. It was so unlike my Laundry Guy who answered the phone with a "Huh?" and scribbled a lot.

The online laundry man returned to the phone and said, "We don't service that neighborhood." I felt crushed.

I sulked. The laundry bag got fuller. I bought new underwear rather than have the dirty ones cleaned. Eventually, I realized it was time to act the part of the grown-up in this relationship.

Laundry Guy could never meet my needs if he didn't know what they were. I separated whites from colors. I itemized each and every article of clothing that went into the bag. I put a copy of the list, along with detailed instructions on washing the whites only with the whites, into the bag and practiced speaking my address in a low, Yemen-like tone.

When he delivered my laundry that night, I smiled. Laundry Guy smiled back. He chatted a bit. He offered to buy me my own laundry if I'd marry his brother. I declined. He mentioned credit problems and service notices from ConEd. I helped him translate the bills from Corporate-Speak into a kind of Brooklyn-ese. Together we filled out loan applications, putting imaginary numbers into blanks where estimates of income should have gone. I peeked in the bag at my whiter whites. He smiled again. I realized he had bigger problems than women who screamed addresses at him.

COLUMBUS Day and Yom Kippur landed on the same day, giving most of the neighborhood a day off. Late in the morning, my landlady came down and tentatively knocked on my door. She and I kept a safe, tenant-landlord distance, which allowed her to make mother-like comments about my hair and general well-being, but it was unusual for her to be standing at my door and she looked a little awkward. She was dressed nicely and had on her wig instead of the scarf she wore to cover her hair while in the house. She asked me if I would do them a favor. If I would push her elderly mother-in-law's wheelchair to the synagogue. With all work banned on Yom Kippur, none of the family would be able to do it themselves.

I said, "Yes" and felt more excited about the request than I thought I should. I had lived in the neighborhood for over a year and was still the outsider. I had grown used to the kosher pizza place that wouldn't put meat on the cheese. And the counter guy at the bagel place, who made a point of not touching my hand when giving me change. There were signs up advertising for a daily *minyan* at the local deli and I had learned to shop for my dairy and my meat at separate stores. There had once been some confusion about where the house's front door was, and I had answered my bell to find seven Orthodox

Jewish teenagers staring at me in my cut-off shorts and t-shirt with no bra underneath. I know they didn't mean to, but they laughed before gathering themselves enough to ask where the rabbi's door was.

My landlord's youngest son would sometimes sit behind my bedroom wall when I brought lovers home. I knew he was there because he would play his guitar. I didn't know if he was trying to drown out the sounds of my sins, or if he wanted to cover up his own. I wondered if he waited for me to walk up the pathway late on Saturday nights. I wondered if he hoped as much as I did that I would have someone with me when I came home.

I didn't know the songs he played. They were all in Hebrew and unfamiliar to me. But I couldn't even begin to guess what they might mean. I imagined him — an arm's-length away from me — dressed in his sharply-pressed white shirt and creased black pants. Yarmulke pinned on his brown hair. A foot propped up on his stool to hold his guitar properly. I imagined that he was playing just for me.

I never told my lovers about the music until it began. They were always caught by surprise. I wanted to see how they would respond. They asked why I put up with it. They asked why I didn't move. Why I didn't complain. Why I wasn't bothered by his presence.

I wondered what they thought I was putting up with.

I liked the certainty of it; his music was always there. I liked how the chords grew louder as I did. I liked how the music meant I never had to worry or give thought to my landlords overhearing my Saturday nights. I liked how his music added an audible element of the ancient to sweaty nights and tangled sheets.

The entire family fascinated me and I thought that pushing the grandmother to synagogue would give me a glimpse into their world.

We talked on the way over. They told me about Yom Kippur. At the entrance to the synagogue, the family took over and led their grandmother inside. I walked home alone.

My lawyer was my landlord's daughter. I could sometimes hear her yelling at her mother. She was younger than I was and wore much more eyeliner. She left a message on my machine telling me I was divorced. She said she had the papers in her office. I started crying.

I felt free. My shoulders felt light. I wanted to run up to strangers on the street and tell them that according to the State of New York, I was a free woman. I had my name back. I was me again. I called Rachel and she told me to meet her at the subway stop in her neighborhood. When I stepped off the Q train, the conductor saw me smiling and as the train was moving out of the station he yelled, "Have a most excellent night!" I blew him a kiss and he waved his way into the tunnel.

Rachel met me on 7th Avenue and brought me flowers. She bought me champagne at dinner and the busboy wished me well. I practiced signing my new, old name over and over on the tablecloth. The next day at work, my favorite coworker changed the nameplate on my cubicle and brought me a Junior's Cheesecake. It made me cry more. It was the first time I told anyone at work that I had left my husband. I hadn't wanted to tell them, but I wanted my name to be accurately reflected on my business cards.

The divorce decree had given me my maiden name back but I still didn't know who I was or what I wanted.

I kept looking into the eyes of the women I had been dating all summer. I kept wondering, "Are you it? Are you what I'm looking for? Will you hold me when I cry and laugh with me at the CVS when I need body glitter at 2 a.m.? Will you understand when I say it's been a hard day and buy me Ben and Jerry's? Would you let me wander through the stacks of books at the Strand and drink with me at the Astor Lounge? Would you go to Coney Island with me and buy cotton candy? Would you let me press my cheek into your blue wool coat and not ever tell me that you had to leave?

I listened to the music that a girl in Boston told me I should buy,

I drank my Jack and Coke and wondered why I persisted in placing personal ads and meeting those women. I wondered why I told my story over and over and watched their eyes drift to the side when I mentioned the divorce, their gaze shift when my accent deepened. They turned away when my lowly bachelor's degree surfaced and my cubicle took center stage.

I wondered. I wondered what it was I was looking for.

I thought I'd know the answer once I was done "coming out," whatever that meant. Someone mentioned the phrase, "gay lifestyle" to me, as in, "we don't want them leading the Boy Scouts and promoting their gay lifestyle." I couldn't get the phrase out of my head. I wanted to know if I led a gay lifestyle. If I really were gay or just pretending. I wondered if the Boy Scouts would keep me out of their troops if I had been a boy. Did I work as "a gay" in the cubicle? I did manage to sneak a reference to domestic partnership benefits into the newsletter, so maybe so. I kept track of one of my afternoons to see if any of it sounded like a gay lifestyle.

5:15 p.m.

Left the cubicle. Refused to get cash from my own bank. Thought I had enough. Walked seven blocks to pick up my mail. There were three birthday cards, one bill and two hometown newspapers. I took the F train to the Q and read a book. I contemplated sentence structure and wondered if I should let an older woman have my seat. I let out a sigh of relief when she found one on her own.

6:07 p.m.

I wondered why the Museum of Modern Art workers were striking. Developed ideas for my own cable access show. Listened in on a conversation about living in St. Louis versus Staten Island.

6:31 p.m.

I got off at my stop. I wondered if I needed cat food. I told myself, "no." I reminded myself that I wouldn't be able to buy cat food again until Friday. I decided I still didn't need it. I stopped at the grocery and bought two whole tomatoes, a box of cherry tomatoes, a box of Harvest Wheat things, a small container of Hellman's mayonnaise, a bottle of seltzer, Spaghetti O's with meatballs, Pepperidge Farms light wheat bread, a chunk of gouda cheese, two pears and decided against the pickled herring. The total was $18.75.

7:16 p.m.

I stopped at the dry cleaners. It was $9.75 for two pairs of slacks and a shirt. I was out of cash and I still hadn't purchased any meat. I stopped at the ATM and agreed to the $1.50 surcharge for having been too stubborn to get cash in the city. My bank balance was $300 greater than I thought. Stopped at the meat market and purchased one pound of bacon and a package of what promised to be "hot ham." The total was $4.80.

7:31 p.m.

Began the wait for the bus. Contemplated walking home with three grocery bags and the dry cleaning. Cursed the fact that I had purchased the heavy seltzer, canned goods and fruit. Continued waiting for the bus. My feet hurt. Wondered if I had scissors at home that would be strong enough to cut my shoes off.

7:52 p.m.

The bus arrived. I dug for my Metrocard. If my arms collapse should I save the meat or the dry cleaning?

8:01 p.m.

I arrived home and fell into the apartment. I forgot to put away the groceries and I let my dry cleaning hang on the back of the front door.

I decided the Boy Scouts probably couldn't use a lightweight like me after all.

 chapter

13

MY TIME at Mega was winding up. The head of investor relations told my coworker that he couldn't believe our department was letting me go. He said,

"She's one of the nicest, most professional, most intelligent people in the department."

I wrote it down so I would remember that someone important had once said something nice about me. My boss was away from the office and changed his voicemail to tell people to call me with any problems. He mispronounced my name in the message. I had worked ten feet away from the man for two years and he still couldn't get my name right. The best part though, was that he got my extension wrong too. My phone never rang and I sat back in my chair with my hands behind my head.

I wanted to always feel as confident as I did when I was at work. But Mega wasn't getting me where I wanted to go. I wanted a comfortable life. I wanted a partner and a job that paid well, didn't morally bankrupt me and didn't interfere with my after-5 reality. I wanted to come home and make soup with the woman I loved and carve a pumpkin. On alternate Thursday nights I thought I might like to go out to a bar with my friends. From time to time I'd be a person who would consider taking a class in something.

I wanted to be the person who always chose to take the bus rather than fly or take the train because it was just a more interesting experience and because while the Port Authority sold beef patties, and Penn Station didn't. I wanted to look forward to phone calls from my mother. I wanted to be able to easily tell people I was gay. I wanted to blush less.

I tried to rationalize my life. To prove to myself that not only did I exist, but that it was okay that I existed. I spent my nights painting my nails black in some sort of corporate girl nod to the power of anarchy. I carefully wiped off the excesses with cotton swabs and polish remover. I pored over tattoo designs confident that if I found just the right one I could tap into an inner rebellious power and would be able to show it to the outer world.

I made people laugh to prove that I was more than a Kentucky education. I typed memos to leave some proof of my abilities. I pet my cat to show my heart still worked. And every morning. I crossed over the Manhattan Bridge. And ran smack into the skyline. I would buy a cup of coffee and flow into the rush of the commuters. I took rather long strides. And I attempted to remember that I was me.

I was flesh and blood and I existed.

I read Homer and Langston Hughes and I could find the power in them both. I was friends with right-wing fundamentalists who tried to save my soul through the power of the word of God, and with East Coast liberals who tried to save my mind through the power of political correctness. They were both right and they were both wrong.

I was the Quaker who marked Jewish holidays and prayed to Catholic saints. I lit candles and burned incense and thought about going to Mass from time to time.

I was the corporate chick who found power in a power suit and in having enough to donate to the local anarchists. I would shake my fist at the powers of class and government and society while wearing designer tights and jewelry from Tiffany's.

I tried to distract myself from the uncertainties and the questions by developing an incredible crush on a woman who was in a writing class I was taking. She was from Israel and I had a fantasy of her serving in the army. She would wear these jeans and this belt that I couldn't take my eyes off. Sweet Jesus, she wore that belt. I brought extra clothes to work with me so I could change before I saw her. I didn't want her to think I was a complete drone. I ran into her at the pizza place before class. We chatted. I felt like a 12-year-old. I wanted to pick her up. I wanted to make her laugh. I wanted to know what made her cry.

She asked about the cheesecake box I was carrying. I told her it was a leftover from an office party. She asked what the event was. I told her it was my happy divorce cake. She smiled. I blushed. I told her I was on a sugar high from the cheesecake and giddy from the divorce. We went to class.

A guy who had been in the class had been asked not to come back. That night, he was standing by the door explaining in great stalker detail why he was no longer in the class. Stalkers are like that. I mean, they think you care. After class started, he pressed on the door's buzzer for an eternity. The instructor called the cops. They came in and asked some questions. Once the cop realized that stalker man had been promised a refund he hadn't yet received, he reduced the entire situation – barging at the door, leaving threatening voice-mails, harassing people on the sidewalk – down to one simple sentence.

"Oh. So it's a money issue."

Which surprised me, because the whole time I thought it was an aggressive, angry stalker issue.

I hadn't expected that kind of anger to find me in Brooklyn. To come into the class I was taking. That night, I was hyper-aware of everything – of everyone in the room and my place in it. My face kept getting red. In discussions, I spoke exactly at the middle. Never the first to speak, never the last. I made very pointed remarks and I stated them very confidently. I talked in clipped and soft tones. I kept the detail to a minimum so that I wouldn't go overboard compared to anyone else. I revealed enough and not too much and I was aware. Hyper-aware of every movement every sound.

I tried to make myself perfect. I sat in the wood chair and not the soft one, so someone else could be comfortable. I was in corporate clothes, so I sat with my legs wide apart so I'd look comfortable and at ease. When someone talked, I put my arm on the back of my seat and appeared interested.

My tongue was glued to the roof of my mouth. My toes curled under tightly. My eyes glazed over from keeping them wide open in feigned interest.

I felt like the power he had over me was never going to leave.

I had a friend – a large, burly, Ukrainian man – walk with me past the edges of my former prison. It was the only way I could screw up the courage to move on, to reclaim the city for myself. In my mind, I had roped off an entire area of Manhattan around my old apartment, where he still lived and where I might have run into him. From the Bowery to Broadway and from Broome to Houston was his. I entered it only with the protection of acquaintances and it gave me chills in the 96-degree heat of a New York summer. I saw the pay phone that had been my link to the outside world. I used to sneak out of the apartment on errands and use that pay phone to call anywhere I could. I had scribbled far-away friends' phone numbers on an old envelope I kept in my bag. Whenever I could sneak away, I'd call one of those numbers. Once when I got out, he thought I had been gone too long and came stalking down the street to find me. I had to stuff the phone card away, make a quick goodbye and pretend. Pretend I hadn't been calling out.

I was slowly reclaiming myself. It was time to reclaim my maiden name with the State of New York's Department of Motor Vehicles. On one of my lunch hours, I took the train to Herald Square and up to the 8th floor. I told the guy at the info counter I needed to change my name. He waved me into a line. I stood there for 15 minutes. I realized I hadn't filled out a form. I realized this would probably require a form. I went back. It was a different guy. Of course I needed a form.

I waited in line another 40 minutes before handing the woman at the counter all of my ID. She studied it.

"Do you have anything else?"

I explained that I had handed her a divorce decree stating in no uncertain terms that the State of New York, her employer, said that I was me. That my maiden name was, in fact, mine. Wasn't that good enough? If the state said I was me, shouldn't the state believe I was me? I looked at her and said,

"I am me."

She went to ask her supervisor if I was me. He nodded. It was approved. According to a divorce decree from the State of New York, a birth certificate from the State of Missouri and various forms of I.D. from the States of Kentucky and Tennessee, and on the power of a nod from a guy in the DMV, I was declared legally me.

I paid my three dollars and left.

I went into the city to watch the first of the World Series games between the Yankees and the Mets. Rachel had gathered a collection of people to see the game with and I wanted to go out. I got dressed. Stretch boots up to the knee, black tights, black skirt with a slit up the thigh, and a shimmery blue shirt. There was body glitter. 'Cause it just seemed a body glitter kind of night. The bartender pointed me to my friends when I walked in the door.

I had spent the whole night talking to a guy-friend of Rachel's. We drank and ate and we talked. We talked through the game. It ended after twelve innings and I didn't even notice who won. The second he had walked through the door and sat at our table, I had turned to Rachel and said,

"God. He's hot."

He was my height and thin. He had black hair, a goatee, brown eyes and a slightly bored look around the edges of his turned down mouth. I imagined he drank a lot of vodka.

We had been having one of those conversations. One of those back-and-forth types of exchanges where you know the other person is purposefully trying to outwit you. It was a game and I was in the groove that night. He told me I was cynical.

"You don't know the half of it."

He laughed at all my jokes. I kept him on his toes. He entered the conversation more than he thought he should. I talked a lot about my past girlfriends. I talked about the crush I had on the girl in my class. I crossed and uncrossed my legs. I wanted him to see the space where my boots ended and my skirt began. I watched his eyes moving along the seams.

I kept them moving.

The game ended and he walked me to the train. I walked faster than he did to prove that I could. He ran to catch up with me. He followed me into the Herald Square subway station and stood next to me on the platform. I was drunk and it was late and I knew I looked good. He put his hand on the small of my back. He leaned in and I thought to myself, *Am I going to let him do this?*

I shut my eyes. And I did. Let his tongue in my mouth and mine in his and I kept my eyes shut.

He asked, "Do you want to go to my place?"

I kissed him back and said, "I think that'd be fun."

I wanted to see what it would be like. I wanted to find out what would happen. I wanted to know if I could make a man do what I wanted him to do. I wanted to find out once and for all if I had been deluding myself by dating women.

We fumbled in his apartment and he kept kissing me. He claimed to be a painter. He had large, bizarre paintings of ex-girl-friends covering his walls. I noticed he included himself in a good bit of them and I declined to wonder what that meant about his personality. At one point, he mumbled the required line, "I'm just not ready for a relationship."

I laughed, looked at him and said, "You know I'll never have a relationship with you, right? I'm just here to have sex."

He told me I wasn't giving him any breaks.

"I don't have to."

He stopped trying to get me to act like the girls he usually brought home and opened his sofa bed. He pulled me onto the sheets and kissed me again. He was different from Kim. He was nothing like Roxanne. I kissed him back and wondered what the difference was.

I realized the difference was that I didn't care about him.

I didn't care about how he was touching me or if I was touching him in any way he wanted. I didn't care if he wanted to talk to me or thought I was hot. I didn't care if I came and I really didn't care if he came. I thought a lot about the fact that it had been almost two years since I had a dick inside of me and I realized I didn't care about that either. I just liked to sleep with girls better.

He finished what he was doing and made sure I was taken care of. It was too late to go home, so I fell asleep. I woke to him painting in another room. I kept my eyes closed because I needed to process. I got the impression that he was coming in and looking at me to use me as some kind of model. I didn't want to confirm that, so I kept my eyes shut. I asked myself if I really wanted to be there. I couldn't think of a reason to leave and I was finding reasons to stay. I noticed how he took the room to himself. How his personality filled all the spaces. I wondered how other girls could deal with that. How they kept from making themselves small in the face of those paintings and that personality. That maleness.

He started to talk about his past relationships and how they had gone sour. I asked him why. He looked at me and said,

"I'm just too nice a guy."

It was all I could do to not laugh at him. He actually believed it.

"You're not too nice a guy. You just want sex without a commitment."

He had no reply.

Two days after I left his apartment, the boy called. He left a message while I was at work. I thought that was pretty genius on his part. The requisite follow-up call, without having to actually talk to me. It was nicely done.

The boy's phone call coincided with my last day at Mega. I cleaned out my desk and carried home all the notepads printed with my name and work number. I had the exit interview and turned in my IDs and my corporate credit card. I hugged the coworkers good-bye and they gave me the same gold earrings every departing female contestant gets.

I went to class that night and continued to swoon after Crush Girl. During break, she mentioned she wouldn't be at the last class the coming week. I realized I had to make my move. I followed her to her subway station mumbling, "Oh, I have to go home this way tonight."

I turned up the charm. I talked a lot about my cubicle and made her laugh. We discussed the Cyclone. When we reached the F train, she turned around and said the words I had been waiting for, "We should do lunch sometime."

I refrained from giggling uncontrollably and said, "That would be so much fun."

We exchanged numbers and I skipped down the subway steps.

I was not nearly as calm and collected when it came to the boy. He left more messages and I hadn't returned any of them. He had also called a friend of Rachel's to make sure things "weren't weird."

I called the boy back. Crush Girl's winks and smiles had made me feel powerful. I thought I could answer whatever questions the boy would throw at me. He said, "We should hang out sometime. Go find a bar or something. What are you doing Friday?"

"Nothing."

"Good. I'll meet you at the F train in Carroll Gardens."

He hung up and the date was set before I realized what had happened. I had agreed to go out with the boy. Again.

chapter
14

I GOT all stupid and called Crush Girl. I called at a time I knew she wouldn't be home because I wanted to contact her, but didn't have the courage to talk to her one-on-one. I left a really long and stupid and rambling message, the upshot of which was, "ummm-mm.... hrmmmm... we should do lunch."

I giggled uncontrollably at one point and said, "Now I just sound stupid." She called back the next night and left me a message in return. The best part was, she sounded all giggly and stupid too and said she'd really like to do lunch sometime and that she had wanted to call me but hadn't.

The next step, of course, was to actually call her when she might be around, which I finally managed to do. In the course of the conversation, much wit was thrown around about her working "on Wall Street" and me working. Um. In a cubicle.

I played up the fact that in my new job, the dress code shrank from five pages to half a page and I could now wear a t-shirt. I told her I was allowed to listen to a radio at work and she applauded. We set a date for lunch. There was a bit of giggling involved in the negotiations.

I loved working in The World Trade Centers. There are 40,000 workers and 100,000 visitors in the complex every day. The closest "big" town to Possum Trot was Paducah, population 30,000. Paducah was where the mall was and where the nearest restaurant with cloth napkins was found. Paducah was where I went to practice parallel parking and where we went to cruise Nobel Park even though we weren't supposed to cruise the park. Demi Moore and Bruce Willis' oldest daughter was born in Paducah, which is a little-known fact and of little interest to anyone but me. Therefore I tell it to everyone.

Paducah is where I rode my first elevator. In the Dry Goods Store, you had to go to the fourth floor for children's clothes. Paducah was where I bought my confirmation dress when I was in the fourth grade. We were confirmed early because the bishop came from Owensboro only when the class got big enough to warrant such a trip.

Paducah seems like a long time ago and a long way away from the World Trade Centers.

I guess that happens.

It was a relief starting the new job. It was exciting getting away from Mega Mega and into the reinsurance company. My new boss was a woman and had a sarcastic wit to match mine. She had also worked for Mega and we joked about the place as much as we dared. I don't think either one of us wanted to admit that sometimes we actually missed it.

My first day on the job coincided with a ticker tape parade down Broadway to celebrate the Yankees winning the World Series. The company hosted a reception for all its employees. Eating sandwiches and soft drinks, we stared out the windows onto the ticker tape floating below us. We could see the whole thing on television and even the Mets fans seemed a little excited. The ticker tape seemed a good way to mark my first day.

I took my sandwich and soda with me when I went into the bowels of the WTC to get my official building ID. To get to the basement, you had to go through a small unmarked door on the other side of the Ben & Jerry's stand. You had to walk down flights of stairs and sign a huge book. Sometimes they would take the book away and call ten people to have their pictures taken. It was a Monday and it was the first day for a lot of us. I sat in the middle of a crowd of recruits from Price Waterhouse Coopers. They had all been given laptops at orientation and they carried their branded laptop bags proudly.

The guys in charge of handing out IDs had a small black-and-white television in the basement set up so that everyone in the waiting area could see what was going on outside with the ticker tape parade. We sat in the waiting room and watched a grainy image of the Yankees and the Mayor and some guy singing "Take Me Out to the Ballgame" like a moron.

The boy called and invited me to a black-tie event at the Museum of Modern Art. He wanted us to go with Rachel and her husband and another couple. It sounded like a triple date. I focused on the chance to get dressed up, the paintings at MOMA and the free bar. I said "yes" because I had never been to a black-tie anything in Manhattan and I didn't want to miss out.

I wanted to blend in and I wanted to buy the clothes to do it with. Shopping had always seemed a mental exercise in hell. Things had to be purchased and they had to be purchased with the least amount of money possible so as to not have an impact on things like eating and rent. With the raises and promotions at Mega and the salary boost with the new job, I could actually purchase things without the men from Visa busting down my door to carry me away to Visa jail.

As it was, I wasn't blending in well at the new job and being asked to a black-tie event just scared me further. My winter coat was six years old and held together with bobby pins. I had paid a grand total of $50 for it when I still lived in Nashville. The pockets were ripped out and the sleeves were too short.

That was the thing about class and money and trying to pass as someone who belonged in the corporate world. You could hide a lot of things in Kmart clothing and hand-me-downs if you did it right. But there were three things you could never hide with discounts and coupons. Straight teeth, good shoes and a good winter coat – the lack of all three embarrassed me on a daily basis.

I had been right to accept the boy's date to the MOMA event. I got to play dress up in the city. I got to put on my little black dress and my shiny pearl drop earrings and my little pearl barrettes and black tights and black shoes and black shawl and an insane amount of makeup. I got ready at Rachel's and sprayed hairspray everywhere. She put on velvet and taffeta and we twirled in her apartment to a *Dixie Chicks* CD. We admired ourselves in the mirror and then tripped down to the subway on our high heels. We pretended we were pretentious, rich snobs on the N train and stared down anyone who looked as if they might think we were too much taffeta for the N. We came up out of the subway in front of MOMA and we knew we looked fabulous.

The boy played the role of the boy all night. It was something about the combination of boys and girls and playing dress up. We had gender roles to uphold and we both knew our lines perfectly. I stood next to him. I giggled a lot. He kept putting his arm around my waist. At the end of the evening, I put him in the Brooklyn-bound cab with me and Rachel and told him I had to pick my stuff up at Rachel's. I let him believe that I meant to come back to his apartment.

I sat in the middle of the backseat and Rachel leaned her head on my shoulder as I toyed with the boy. She giggled under her breath whenever I told him a half-truth. I wanted to make her laugh more so I played up the game. I let him touch the top of my thigh. I let him rest his hand on my black stocking.

At her apartment, she and I slid out of the car together. I kissed the boy on the cheek. I told the cab driver to hit it and the boy looked confused. I told him he shouldn't make so many assumptions and I followed Rachel inside as the cab and the boy drove away. The next day at work, I downed a lot of Advil and tried to forget that any of it had happened.

The boy wouldn't give up. He pissed me off by not respecting my boundaries. I told him I just wanted sex, not a relationship, and he kept pushing it. He kept calling and inviting himself over to my place for dinner. He said he was cooking and he dragged me with him to the grocery store. Somewhere along the way, I asked him to stay over. It seemed like a good idea at the time.

He made dinner and we watched television and I led him into my bedroom. He pushed me on the bed and mumbled, "Why do you do this? Why do you look so hot and lead me on? Why did you invite me over?"

I was confused. I didn't want to answer, because I didn't want to think about the fact that I had invited him over. I wanted to think that he had appeared on my doorstep on his own. That I had nothing to do with the exchange or the relationship or the kissing. That things just happened and I just happened to go along with them. I didn't want to know that I had anything to do with it.

The next morning I followed him back to his place. I had never been very good at being alone and I didn't want to sit in my apartment with only the burden of my actions. On the way to his place, he bought me tulips and ice cream.

I wasn't getting it. I didn't like how I felt when I was around the boy. I didn't like how I let his opinions flow over mine. I didn't like how I smiled more than I talked. I didn't like how I made myself small around him and I didn't like how I didn't feel a damn thing for him.

The next day, the boy called me at work and left a voicemail. He called again at 8:30 p.m. He was upset.

"I'm not used to spending a whole weekend with someone and then not getting a return phone call."

He said he couldn't be anything more than friends. I said, "I thought that's what we said all along."

He feigned innocence and acted hurt. He pretended that he was dumping me. I told him that he should try not calling me again. I hung up, put on some flannel pajamas and took a Tylenol PM. I called Rachel and told her the whole story. She taught me how to say, "Screw you" to a boy and I went to sleep.

Two weeks after he spent the night at my apartment he was back together with his ex-girlfriend. Rachel helped me drown any feelings I might have over it by going to a bar on Avenue B.

I KEPT looking in the mirror, examining myself. I didn't know how I had come to look so old. Like an adult. At work I would write bitchy emails and joke with vendors who asked me out. People wanted my opinion. When I spoke forcefully enough, they would listen. The CEO sent me email. The chairman of the board dropped by to tell me jokes. I was in charge of projects and I had to remind myself to do what was in my job description instead of the clerical functions I was used to.

My boss and I often dressed alike. We were both slightly obsessive and very into schmoozing. We had short blonde hair and the same complexion. We sometimes wore our powder blue sweaters and gray pants on the same day. She called them trousers, which is how I knew there were still some differences between us.

She had nice nails. I liked to watch her maneuvering for a future promotion. I liked seeing how I could fit into that plan of hers. I liked that she was bringing me along. On the way home one night, I stopped and got a manicure. I wanted my boss' office.

My boss decided our company needed a banner. Something to hang behind a podium and use at press events.

I was put in charge of obtaining said banner. I obtained dimensions and scouted the city. It's what I was paid to do. I called a hundred banner guys and found the perfect one in Tribeca. He quoted me a price and I joked with him. He quoted me a lower price. I joked more and told him I wanted to see samples. He gave me directions. When I got there, I made him laugh. I brought out all my best moves. I tilted my head and turned up the Southern accent.

He cut his price by half and upped the quality of the material by a hundred percent. He was originally from Poland and proud that he was now a citizen of the United States. He took an American flag off his desk and handed it to me.

"This is for you. To remember me by."

I kept getting lost on the way back to the office. I kept looking up to find the towers and orient myself. I kept moving south and kept my eyes on the sky so I wouldn't lose sight of where my office was. I carried my American flag into the World Trade Center and set it in a pencil holder on my desk.

I didn't want to forget my banner guy. His name was Henry.

I used all the charm I had to keep things moving in my new job. I got major bonus points for getting a video duplicated in a three-hour time frame. I was mostly able to do it based on the cache of my company's World Trade Center address and the fact that the duplication guy was in the building where I used to pay my rent. We joked about all of that and he threw in the rush service for free.

Unfortunately, the charm wasn't working with anyone who actually worked with me inside the company. I was undergoing a three-week-long power struggle with the guy in the information services department who had been in charge of the company's intranet until I was hired. He was trying to keep control and wouldn't give me access to his servers. The server was the least of my annoyances. The biggest annoyance was that the guy's wife had designed the intranet and I was in the process of redesigning it. Because it sucked.

Every time I made a change, he would tell me that I was wrong. I was making a hell of a lot of changes and we were having a lot of "you're wrong" conversations.

I tried being polite.

"You and I have different priorities."

That's how I would phrase it. I was afraid one day I would phrase it by pouring coffee over his head.

My blood pressure was on its way to reaching the boiling point. The IS guy was bearing the brunt of it. One of the bosses wanted a press release put on the intranet before the office closed, at 1 p.m., for the Thanksgiving holiday. I got the release at 11:30 a.m. I still didn't have access to the servers and I couldn't get the rights to put the article up. The big boss called me at 1:05 p.m.

"I am really disappointed that this didn't go up before now."

I walked into his office and "relayed my concerns" about the numbers of people involved in projects like putting up a simple press release. He smiled and nodded as I laid the blame accordingly. He said he'd do what he could to get me the tools I needed to do my job.

"That's all I need," I said.

"Have a good holiday," he said.

I planned a big Thanksgiving celebration. My sister flew up from Nashville and my friends Kevin and Lisa were driving in from Baltimore. Before they arrived, I took my sister to Brighton Beach because I took everyone I loved to Brighton Beach to judge how much they understood me. My sister liked the sunset. She complained about the cold. I liked hearing my boots on the boardwalk. I bought huge coffee mugs and garish, horrible salt and pepper shakers at the Russian store under the elevated subway platform. The shakers were a pink sparkly glaze with a colonial man and woman on the front. They matched my kitchen perfectly.

We came home and ordered pizza and I tried to figure out when

I could call Crush Girl. I wanted to pour her coffee in my new mugs. I almost saved the shopping bags they came in because they said "Brighton Beach." I thought I might want a souvenir to remember. To prove I had been to Brighton Beach. And then I remembered that I lived three stops from the beach. I could go anytime I wanted.

When Kevin and Lisa got in, I was still trying to make the apartment perfect. I told myself to stop vacuuming. I told myself to stop eyeing the baseboards. Kevin had to order me to stop cleaning the kitchen. I kept telling him that I'd been well-trained by the patriarchy. Truth of the matter was, I had a hard time not trying to make everything perfect.

Even with my sister and two dear friends around me for Thanksgiving dinner, I felt alone. I had lost my ability to cook, so we all shared Chinese takeout and a bottle of Dom Perignon. We toasted to "good friends," and I continued with the alone, alone, alone chorus. We got up Saturday and laughed and giggled and went to Ellis Island. I became overwhelmed and hid in the gift shop. We got off the boat and ran into two older ladies from Wisconsin. They were wondering how to get to the Empire State Building. I told them to follow me. They laughed at our jokes and we laughed at theirs. I explained to them that they would not die by taking the subway. When they told me the highlight of their trip had been a visit to St. Patrick's Cathedral, I wrote out directions for them to get to Old St. Patrick's, as well.

At the Prince Street subway stop, someone called out my name. It was a coworker. We discussed the election and made a woman sitting near us giggle despite her better judgment. We had Indian food on 6th street and stopped to spend far too much money at St. Mark's Bookstore.

My guests and I went back to Brooklyn and contemplated bar choices. I suggested my favorite bar, the Rising. It was agreed. We walked in and standing in the corner was Crush Girl. I giggled a lot. She hugged me. I was glad I was wearing what I was wearing. I was glad my hair looked good. We went back to our respective corners to discuss the interaction with our friends.

By the time I got through my second beer, a large portion of her group had left. I sauntered over and sat next to her on the couch. We talked. She touched my knee said,

"You're going to call me, right?"

"Yes."

The company's CEO called me from Paris. I was confused when the call came in. At one point in my life, I had worked in Paris, Tennessee, and the CEO's accent wasn't sounding Southern. He had an urgent project for me. I had no idea how I came to have the life I was leading. At one point, my highest ambition had been to work at a community newspaper in Kentucky and raise children. I thought I might live in a nice doublewide and have a husband who wore Levis to work. I couldn't remember how I had come to be sitting in the World Trade Center wearing power suits and getting calls from the CEO.

My mother was sending me emails with pictures of dressers in them. She wanted to give me furniture for Christmas. It sounded good to me since I didn't have any furniture other than the sofa I had taken with me from the marriage, the bed I had bought immediately after, the orange recliner my landlords had given me, and the entertainment center I got from Rachel. My socks and unmentionables were piled into cardboard boxes that lined my bedroom floor.

I finished off the project for the CEO with a round of "great work!" that he very appropriately copied my supervisor on. I finished the final announcement of an employee contest that was set to go out the next day in New York, Chicago, San Francisco, Mexico City and Miami. I sat down with the chairman of the board and drafted bits of this and that in the form of memos that he needed. I made changes to the intranet. I booked a caterer for the holiday party. I chose chicken sate and spring rolls for the appetizers because I like them better than quiche. I arranged to have a temp come in and help me mail out 200 leather-bound company calendars to the appropriate clients.

I was still trying to get comfortable. Learning how to be content in my new life. I felt tense a lot. I went to sleep tense. I woke up in the mornings stiff. I clenched my jaw an awful lot. I thought out every phrase before I allowed myself to utter it. The head of marketing came and sat in my cube. He wanted to get my opinion on how he should approach the CEO to get something done that he knew the CEO wouldn't want to do. I asked the appropriate questions. I gave the appropriate advice.

He didn't know that I was planning each and every response as he was talking to me. I did that a lot. I didn't know how to stop. My cubicle was the only place where I knew what all the rules were. I felt sure and steady inside the three fabric walls. My cubicle had been the only spot where I had been safe during my marriage and thinking inside the box was my specialty. I wondered what I wasn't allowing myself to say. What I was keeping behind that clenched jaw.

The night I packed to leave my marriage was the first great emptiness I had allowed myself to feel. I sat sobbing in the middle of the apartment, wrapping china in newspaper. Ink-stained fingers wiping away tears. I paid attention to no details other than the desire to get away. The emptiness was huge. I was piling it all into boxes and sealing it with masking tape. I was leaving the only life I knew. I had tried to fill myself with matching place settings and a gold band. I stripped all that away. I put it into the boxes and waited for the movers.

I knew I was supposed to be just fine on my own. I knew that I wasn't supposed to want someone in my life, but I did.

I was excited to find out that I knew exactly what kind of eggs I liked. I had been watching a movie about a woman who was scared to commit. Scared to get involved. Scared to be in a relationship. A friend of hers thought the crux of her problem might be that she was so wrapped up in the lives of the men that she dated, that she didn't even know how she liked her eggs.

I knew that I liked my eggs sunny-side up. I liked my yolks to run around my hash browns. I liked to mix my Jimmy Dean sausage patty into the swirl and I rather enjoyed sopping the whole deal up with a piece of whole wheat toast covered in butter and strawberry preserves.

I wondered if knowing how I liked my eggs meant that I was ready to be in a relationship. If I had healed enough.

I took the elevator down at lunch and purchased a powder blue coat for myself. It was wool like Laura's had been. This one though, was mine.

I was beginning to remember to stretch when I woke up in the mornings. Long stretches that I could feel in every ounce of my body. I would stretch wide and long and it felt good. I would pull out every muscle and wiggle my toes.

My cat Alice would hear me stirring and leap onto the bed with a little meow. We did it every morning.

Alice would snuggle in my lap while I worked on the home computer. She lay on the couch with me to watch television. She'd lie on her back with her four paws sticking straight up. Then she would stretch her back, and frequently fall off the couch. She would land on her feet and immediately start licking one paw. Calmly.

I tried to be more like Alice.

Alice watched a lot of squirrels. She had been known to chase bouncy balls. She attempted to drown catnip toys in her water bowl. She would become obsessed with the kitty litter and keep scraping and scraping and scraping until I thought I'd go insane. I would let her finish it, though. I knew how I got when someone interrupted my baseboard cleaning.

I wanted to be Alice when I grew up.

Alice attacked Hershey's kisses as if they were evil. She would carry them from room to room by their tags. Sometimes she would drop them and bat them around a bit. Frequently she drowned them in her water bowl. Alice sat in windows a lot. Whenever a bus passed, her ears perked up. She hid under the bed when the Domino's guy rang the bell. Every afternoon at 6 p.m., Alice sat in the kitchen window and watched me come up the walk. She greeted me at the door by lying on her back and stretching so that I could rub her tummy.

I was always careful not to step on her as I came in the door. I rubbed her tummy and asked her how her day was. Alice couldn't meow properly and everything came out a meep. I took my coat off and came into the living room. Alice stretched again. I lay down on the floor and stretched, too. We nudged one another's head and said, "I love you."

Alice was teaching me to be at ease at home and it was carrying over into the world.

I finally went out on a real date, not just drinks after work, with Crush Girl. And I relaxed. I strutted and I moved. We went to see some angsty lesbian theater. I felt like I belonged there.

We walked to dinner afterward. After that, we went for Krispy Kremes and talked over coffees. I invited her out to a bar and she said she had to go home. I walked her to her subway station and hugged her good-night.

I wanted to be able to run. I wanted to be able to stretch my legs out gracefully and pound my feet into the pavement. In grade school, I used to watch this girl named Donna run. She was taller than I was, and I was tall. Donna was loud and abrasive and tall. She didn't get noticed. Donna never cared because she could *run*. Her ability to run was discovered one day during phys-ed class in elementary school. The coach had us run. We all watched Donna.

She was gorgeous. She'd stretch out her legs so perfectly and hold her head high. I heard the coach whisper what we were all thinking.

"Beautiful."

I always wanted to be able to run. Instead, I would stretch out timidly. I was tense and I was tight and it showed. I couldn't run. I could walk exceedingly well. I was a great walker. I could stride like no one's business. I wore proper shoes for walking. I knew exactly where I was going even when I didn't.

I watched a man running for a bus one night after work. He had on a long black overcoat, gray pants and dress shoes. He was tall and had closely-cropped hair. He wanted to catch a bus and he ran. Down Broadway. Past Wall Street. Toward Trinity Church. Through throngs of commuters. Past white twinkly lights and open public spaces and racks of red *Village Voice* newspaper stands. He ran.

He gave no thought to cars whirring past him or crowds pushing against him. He didn't pause and wonder if his shoes would give out and cause him to slip. Thoughts of a pothole or sidewalk crack never entered his reality. He stretched out his legs and put down his feet squarely and surely and confidently. I wanted to whisper. I wanted to say.

"Beautiful."

 chapter

16

I FOUND an express bus that would take me directly home. I would never have to switch trains or buses again. I felt so together. So solid. I vacuumed and I dusted. I washed the dishes. I paid all the bills and filled out a change of address form. I decided to give up my post office box. I wanted my mail sent to my apartment like everyone else. I wanted to stop hiding. I wanted my magazine subscriptions to say "Brooklyn" on them. I wanted my name to match my location. I wanted to be secure in who I was, where I was.

I remembered to take a poetry book with me each morning. I had a coffee and a homemade sausage biscuit before I left. I went to sleep each night in flannel pajamas and under warm, handmade quilts. I left my slippers by the foot of my bed at night and I put them on every morning.

I stayed home most nights. I pet my kitty and read. I watched television and I talked on the phone. I hummed Christmas carols. I looked around. And I felt proud.

I had almost stopped being tense, but in the process, I was on the verge of becoming an Agnes.

Becoming an Agnes had been a great fear of mine. Agnes worked upstairs. She was a professional assistant. She assisted professionals. In a past economy, Agnes was called a secretary. She left at 5 p.m. on the dot. Agnes might have worked her way up from the steno pool. She was an office girl and a right-hand woman. She pushed the paper of the paper pushers.

An actual Agnes lived three blocks from me. When I met her, she made sure to let me know that she owned her own home. She stopped by my cubicle with the assistant to the CEO. Just to chat. Agnes never traveled alone. She referred to the bodega on our shared corner as the "quickie mart." I liked to think this meant there were still some differences between us.

I overheard two Agneses in line for the express bus talking about their bosses. Apparently, at the Agneses' law firm, the bosses don't know how to use Microsoft Word. The Agneses spoke in great detail about how the lawyers couldn't perform the simplest word processing function. The Agneses spoke of phoning London. I figured that this was not a small law firm. These were not small lawyers. One Agnes claimed that a partner in the firm had gotten his first computer a month before. She was proud of him.

"You hear him in there typing away like he knows what he's doing."

The other Agnes and I chuckled. I looked at them and realized I had forgotten to reapply lipstick before leaving the building. When I worked in midtown and took the subway, I put on lipstick once in the morning and that was it. When I started working downtown and taking the express bus, I reapplied lipstick every evening at 5 p.m. Every Agnes on the express bus wore fresh lipstick, because you never knew what was going to happen.

One of the Agneses proved that point when a sharp-looking young Wall Street type asked her where Rector and Greenwich was. She pointed it out. She giggled when he left. She told the other Agnes, "I just about said, 'Let me show you where Rector is!'"

The three of us giggled like we were 16. I put on more lipstick.

Catching the express bus was causing me to time out my life in minute increments. I began to view drinks after work as a great inconvenience — it would mean missing my express bus and taking the subway. I looked for ways to create more time in my day. I saved leftovers to take for lunch. I tried to go to bed promptly at 10 p.m. I purchased my holiday cards a good month before the actual holiday. I made an address list and considered putting it into a mail merge on Microsoft Word.

Tonight I wasn't worried about the express bus. It was the night of the company's holiday party. No one was doing anything in their cubicles and I was sending sexy emails to a girl in Boston. The Agnes who worked upstairs and lived around the corner called to say that her brother could give me a ride home at 9:30, after the holiday party had ended. I wondered what kind of party ended at 9:30. I told her that was fine. I hung up and thought about buying some shoes that were more sensible than the ones I had on. I called Rachel to ask her opinion.

She told me that her husband's holiday party was being held that night too, in a club that was one block from where my company's party would be. We made plans to meet up. I called Agnes back and told her I wouldn't need her brother's ride.

Ours was a holiday party of major geek proportions. I made small talk with the underwriters and claims guys. No one danced well. The French CEO danced with a receptionist from New Jersey. I was introduced to the chairman's wife. I danced with my boss' husband, who was a full foot shorter than both my boss and I. At one point in the evening, 150 underwriters, claims guys and their spouses, formed a conga line around the dance floor. They circled the restaurant twice before giving up.

When the party ended, I called Rachel. Her husband worked for a high-tech company with offices on lower Broadway. They had rented out the hippest club in Manhattan for the evening. There were strobe lights and people carrying multi-colored Cosmos. There were no underwriters or claims guys.

Rachel and I boogied and shimmied. We downed Cosmos and were delighted with ourselves. We were young and beautiful and it was Manhattan. We stood on the furniture and danced under the disco balls and strobe lights. There was a bass beat under it all.

The party broke up. We hailed a cab and went uptown to celebrate the birthday of a friend.

We found our friends at an Irish pub. They bought us a round just for having shown up. We poked each other and giggled a lot. We talked about everything and nothing. The innuendos were flying and we snapped with the night.

I went into the bathroom. I came out of the stall and there was a girl standing at the sink. She was wearing a baby-doll tee and low riding jeans. She had long, curly, tangled black hair. She turned to me and said,

"Do you know who Elizabeth Cady Stanton was?"

I did and I said so.

She led me back to her table. I met her friends and we talked. I made them laugh. We talked about everything and nothing and we were all terribly witty about it. Someone put music on the jukebox. The girl with the curly hair pulled me out of my seat and we started dancing. No one else was dancing. We were dancing. She in her baby doll tee and me in my power suit and black nylons. I pulled her to me because I wanted to make her gasp. She ground herself into me. People at the bar were staring. A group of men in the corner brought us tequila shots. We drank them and kept dancing.

It was Manhattan. It was night. We were young.

We left the bar at 3 a.m. The girl with the curly hair kissed me good-bye. I whispered in her ear,

"Beautiful."

I climbed into a cab with Rachel and her husband and we went to Brooklyn. Rachel told the cab driver to take the Brooklyn Bridge. We didn't want the night to end and the bridge was strung out with white lights. We rolled down the windows and yelled out our names. Our words were frozen in the night and we passed the skyline of Manhattan. Rachel looked at the skyscrapers on the edge of the night and said,

"That's New York. And we get to live here."

 chapter

17

I HAD been emailing a girl in Boston for months. Just after
Thanksgiving, things began to heat up. She began to flirt and I began
to notice. One Saturday she sent me an email with an attachment. It
was a digital picture of her bed. The covers were pulled down and the
morning light spread across the crisp, white sheets. The patchwork
quilt was tangled in sunlight. I stretched my arms over my head. I
could feel that picture in my toes. I wrote her back and told her I was
eating breakfast. That I liked to make myself biscuits on Saturdays
because I could take my time eating them. I could do it properly. I
spread the email out with my Southern drawl and I told her about
pulling the biscuits out of the oven. The were hot and I smothered
them with butter. Real butter. It dripped.

"I like to lick the butter off my fingers before it runs down the
length of my hand."

She emailed back and asked for my phone number.

She called and I lay down on my couch. I let her words slide over
me. She was Southern, too. From Virginia. Her voice had a coastal
drawl that made my back arch and I settled deeper into my couch. I
turned the lights off and put the CD player on. I wrapped myself in a
quilt and blushed. I spoke low and I wanted to say more but I was

patient. I was good. I waited. I sank down into her voice and told her she needed to be in Brooklyn. The Girl in Boston asked when I was free.

"Come down for Rachel's birthday party. It's next week and it's in Manhattan. I'm planning the whole thing and you'll love it."

I gave her directions and she told me to make sure I found a dark corner in the bar before she got there. She wanted to talk to me in person.

On my lunch hour, I went down into the mall under the World Trade Center and bought a black velvet shirt, a pair of dark red and black faux snakeskin pants and a pair of silver hoop earrings for the party. The pants were a size I hadn't seen in 12 years. I pictured The Girl from Boston walking in and seeing those pants and it made me giggle and stumble over my words at the cash register. The Girl's phone calls had caused me to wake up in tangled sheets with the sound of her voice still in my ears and the feeling of her presence in my dreams.

I had been planning Rachel's birthday party for months. I was particularly proud of the email invitation I had sent to 56 of her nearest and dearest:

"It's official. Without having had a recount... despite the complete lack of coverage from CNN... and with absolutely no decisions handed down from upper courts, lower courts or whatever court it was that determined the word "Chad" was a polling term and not just a guy who managed my high school's varsity basketball team...

You're invited to come celebrate the birthday of the completely uncontested Rachel. Join us at the B Bar on Friday, December 15 at 7:30 p.m.

If you have any questions, comments, or ideas for my mom's Christmas present, feel free to email me."

A guy I didn't even know replied to say he would be there and that I gave good email.

I bought $62.47 worth of body glitter, tiaras (four kinds), body stickers, wands (both gold and silver), mardi gras beads, rings and toys for the party. I had never really believed it when people told me you couldn't buy happiness. I knew that you could sure as hell purchase accessories to happiness my friends.

Rachel and I went out for drinks and met up with a guy we both knew. He was having relationship troubles and was really out of sorts. We had dinner and more drinks and he tried to make us laugh. I was feeling New York and Flatbush and the guy wasn't keeping up. He stumbled over his words and couldn't tell a joke. I told him it was no wonder his girlfriend left him.

He looked at me and started to cry.

We split the bill and he left $20 too much. He was drunk and I couldn't persuade him to put it back in his wallet. As we were sliding away from the table, I slid the extra money into my bag. Rachel saw me and laughed. We put on our coats and the guy invited me to a steak dinner. I told him he should think about what he was saying. Rachel and I went back to my apartment.

I was carrying a hundred details in my head at once. I planned a last-minute luncheon for the office and remembered to send out twelve updates to various managers on the United Way campaign. While composing the emails, I was on hold with UNICEF tracking our company's Christmas cards. The ones that should have arrived the day before. I ate my soup. I color-coded the United Way givers by branch office and cross-listed them by category. I filled in charts accordingly. I picked glitter off of my sweater and wondered how one of my Alice's hairs made it onto my desk.

Through it all. I imagined. In detail. How the visit with The Girl from Boston was going to go.

I knew who she was when she walked into the bar but I stayed in my seat. I wanted her to come to me. She did. We hugged and she gave a bottle of champagne to Rachel. I handed her one of the tiaras and she asked me,

"Where's that corner I asked you to track down?"

I pretended I didn't hear her and took her around to talk to my friends. I kept her moving so I could look at her. I had planned Rachel's party and I wanted her to know it. We sat down at the table and she slipped her hand onto my thigh. I handed her a drink. The night went on and the party went on. She looked around at the table full of people talking and she grabbed my hand. It was close to midnight and she had found her dark corner. The Girl from Boston looked at my tiara and she looked at my lips. She looked into my eyes and traced the outline of my chin with her finger. She told me my lipstick was beautiful and pressed her hand into the small of my back. She kissed me.

I kissed her back.

The party started to break up and I asked her if she really wanted to spend the night with her friend who lived in Manhattan, or if she wanted to see Brooklyn. She said she wanted to drive me home.

I didn't own a car and I barely knew the roads in New York City. They were vague descriptions I heard used in traffic reports and they bore no resemblance to the subways and buses I used to get around. I told her to go over the Brooklyn Bridge. We got lost and I started following the subway stations. I figured they would get us close. It was 2 a.m. and we were more lost than I wanted to tell her.

We ended up in Crown Heights and I had to pee. I had been drinking steadily at the party and there was no way I could hold it any longer. I told her to pull over and not talk to anyone. I locked her door and ran into the nearest subway station. It was going to have to do.

She laughed at me when I got back. Told me I was crazy for getting out of a car wearing snakeskin pants in a neighborhood where the fast food places were covered in bullet-proof glass. She pulled me into her to kiss me again and I knew that she understood. Everything.

We made it to my apartment after chasing the B42 bus that ran along Nostrand Avenue, off Flatbush and straight to my apartment. I told her to follow it and when we got in the door I lay down on my couch and I said,

"Come here."

She did and I showed her exactly what her emails and pictures and the light on her bed had done to me. I showed her how her Virginia accent had raced through my mind. I pressed her into the couch and smiled. She held my hips steady with her hands and pressed her lips against mine. Lightly at first. Opened my mouth with her tongue.

"Come here."

Bit her lip. Gently. Pulled at it, tugged at it, showed her my insistence, showed her I wanted her with my mouth. Let my hand. Let my fingertips. Trace the full outline of her onto my couch. Her palms pressed hard on my belly running down running up she moved into me. With fingers and hand and my thighs and her breasts and my everything.

I kept whispering. Kept saying. Demanding. Insisting. Repeating. Kept on wanting her to,

"Come here."

Through the night. In the morning. For the entire weekend.

And she did.

Before she left on Sunday, I took her for a walk along the boardwalk on Brighton Beach and into Coney Island. I wanted to see how she did. If she would get why I loved the boardwalk so much. It was raining and she stopped to kiss me at dusk. She pointed out the fading neon sign of the Cyclone and how the boardwalks rushed against the winter ocean. She looked at me and said, "The whole thing is gorgeously decrepit."

I slipped my arm around her waist and had her walk closer to me. I didn't want her to leave.

She went back to Boston.

I sat in my apartment and tried to keep the feeling of her from ending. I wanted to own it. Keep it as mine. It was raining outside and my arms ached. My legs were sore and my lips were well kissed.

I kept licking them. Trying to taste her.

I had spent the better part of my marriage fading into the wallpaper. I worried that I would never stop doing it. I worried I would never stop trying to press myself into the plaster. I worried it would always be easier, more convenient, more comfortable. To keep myself small.

That weekend, The Girl had shown me that I didn't have to live small. I could come out of the wallpaper and make myself seen.

chapter

18

THE BIGGEST thing I had known as a child was the Kentucky Dam. Kentucky Dam is what backs up the Tennessee River and creates Kentucky Lake, the largest manmade lake in the eastern United States. The lake covers 160,000 acres and stretches south for 184 miles, across the western tip of Kentucky and the width of Tennessee. The dam was built in the late 1930s and early 40s. It is over a mile across and 206 feet tall.

There was a place near Kentucky Dam where you could go and stand on a little hill and look down at the entire dam. That stretch of concrete that held back the rush of the Tennessee River.

After I turned 16, I would drive over to the hill next to the locks. You had to drive across the dam to get to it. If you took your eyes off the road, you felt as if you might fly off into the sailboats below. I would stand on that grassy hill on summer days. And I would breathe in the green of the trees and the grass. The murkiness of the lake water.

That powerful and massive and steady dam was everything of comfort and home and familiarity to me. Unknown and strong and powerful all at once. Solid and still capable of quick movement.

After The Girl left that weekend, I sat in my apartment and listened to the rain. I sipped some coffee and wrapped myself up in a quilt. I felt massive and powerful. Steady and moving and shifting and solid.

The Girl invited me to Boston for Christmas. I said yes and bought a ticket for Greyhound. It snowed the entire four hours it took to get to her.

I rode into the South Station and set my bags down. I looked around and saw her. We hugged and were awkward. I told myself it was the bus ride. We went to her house and she kissed me. We grew less awkward. She brought out a wrapped box and presented it to me. I ripped off the paper.

She bought me a printer.

For one of my birthdays, my dad had gotten me a typewriter. He had been laid off that summer and had worked extra jobs to buy that typewriter. For Christmas eve, The Girl bought me a printer. There was no more awkward.

We went to dinner. I had salmon and ordered a Harpoon. I kept telling myself not to like her so much. I was failing miserably. In the restaurant, they turned the lights down low. We kissed in the car.

It was night and then it was day. We ate breakfast and walked the dog. We lay around on her bed in the morning light. She had planned a dinner party to introduce me to her friends. She cooked. She chopped and she sliced and she diced. She stood in the kitchen and from time to time she came out to the living room to kiss me. I kissed her back.

Her friends came over and there was champagne. There was a fire in the fireplace and nutballs to munch on. Traditional Christmas carols were sung over glasses of wine and carols were twisted around to become jokes about a dominatrix and a loose woman named Rita. There wasn't a straight person in the room. I had never felt so comfortable. It was Christmas Eve.

During the four-hour bus ride back to New York, I contemplated a move to Boston. I imagined reading *The Boston Globe*. I wondered what it would be like to be a Yankees fan in the land of the Red Sox. I thought about jobs and cars and apartments and learning how to drive again. I wondered if I could move from a tomato-based chowder to one that was cream-based. I thought perhaps I could. I almost had myself convinced that was a possibility.

And then the bus turned into Central Park.

I didn't even like Central Park. It was a park for rich people. The city tended to it and rich people donated to it and everyone fusses over it while perfectly gorgeous parks in other areas are ignored.

I hated Central Park because I always got lost in it. I never knew where I could pee. I had been contemplating a life in Boston, and then the bus took a turn through Central Park.

Jesus.

I thought about living in Boston. With a girl I knew I was going to come to love. And I remembered. That the best thing about Central Park. Other than the fact that I loathe it. Is that it's in New York.

And so was I.

Over New Year's Eve, it snowed and The Girl came to visit.

I had fallen in love with her and it scared me. I felt foolish and silly. I was almost positive that I had found the one.

The city had fallen under a blizzard and we watched it unfold on television with the drama that only New York City could produce. The police commissioner advised all criminals to stay indoors. The parks commissioner provided hot chocolate to people sledding in the parks and gave out the best piece of advice I had heard in months,

"Any hill is a good hill. Just beware of the rocks."

The Girl and I went for a walk around the neighborhood. Brooklyn was silent and she made snow angels in strangers' yards. I went to pick up my laundry and the 14-year-old girl working the counter claimed she couldn't find it. I told her to look harder. She said she thought it might be in the van behind the store. I followed her outside to look and she threw snowballs at me. I threw some back and retrieved my clean undies. I told her she should reconsider her attempts at customer service before I tipped her again. My Laundry Guy ran after me to wish me a late "Merry Christmas." I was his one Christian customer. He asked why I hadn't come by to talk to him in awhile. He asked if I was mad. If I had been busy. If I had gotten married. If I was with anyone.

"Oh. You strong girl. You no need anyone. You on your own. You strong girl."

As 2000 moved into 2001, The Girl and I sat on the couch eating a dinner I made. We drank wine; we watched movies; we sat close and we talked.

The Girl gave me a ring. It was a simple, sterling silver ring that she had bought from a street vendor and worn for months. She handed it to me quickly and told me to remember her whenever I was on my own in Brooklyn.

I had no idea what that meant, if anything, but I loved it. I loved the weight of it on my finger. I loved that she gave it to me. I loved that she gave it to me casually. I loved the way she held me. And looked at me and talked to me. I loved the way she let me sing and read cereal boxes to her.

I told her I loved her.

She told me she loved me.

I was still scared.

Every other weekend I rode the bus from New York to Boston to see The Girl. Greyhound is the best choice when you don't have a car and can't afford going Amtrak at $90 a roundtrip. I scrounged around for a Student Advantage card that got me a $20 discount and if I played the schedule right, I could get the bus that featured a free movie on the ride, something I found deeply satisfying.

There came a time when I couldn't stop thinking about The Girl.

I knew I was in love. I liked the way The Girl drove her SUV, shifting gears with this confidence that I don't think she knows she has. The Girl arranged candlesticks on the mantel above her fireplace. She bought two half-cases of Harpoon for Rachel. She wore the same pair of earrings whenever she went out. She once wore a chain. This silver link chain around her neck that I had taken by the teeth one night. The Girl sometimes whistled for her dog and had a favorite cat. I liked the way she lined her grill tools up on the deck. They were parallel to one another and I wanted in on that symmetry.

I loved The Girl.

The Girl came to Brooklyn and we went out to Park Slope. When the night ended, it was midnight and it was sleeting. We walked to the ATM to get cash for the ride home. I stood behind The Girl as she punched numbers, and I pressed my thigh between The Girl's legs. The Girl took out some twenties. I kissed her neck. The fluorescent lights in the ATM lobby glared. We walked outside holding hands. We found a gypsy cab to take us home. I asked the driver the cost.

"We're going to Midwood. Kings Highway and Nostrand. How much?"

"Yo no se. I call the station and ask."

He was speaking in Spanish and I was speaking in some language that only comes around at midnight in Brooklyn when you're in love. The Girl and I sat in the backseat with our thighs pressed together. The Girl tried to make me flirt and I could only focus on how this ride would end. How much this driver would charge and how this situation could go in my favor.

"I have $20. They always charge $15. The cheaper ones charge $12. I know she has at least $20 too, but if I don't get this settled now, he'll screw me later," I whispered to myself.

The Girl looked at me in the backseat of this gypsy cab. She leaned back and smiled. She stopped trying to get me to toss my hair.

She moved her hand down my thigh and she understood where my heart was.

"You belong here. You are beautiful in Brooklyn. You belong here perfectly."

She was right. I did.

I didn't do so well when I was out of my element. It was on one of my Greyhound rides to Boston, one without a movie, that I mentioned to my seatmate that homosexuality was a sin. I said it casually. I had been telling some story about a friend getting pregnant in college.

"Getting pregnant when you're not married is a much bigger sin than being gay."

I caught myself and was able to quickly rationalize to my also-gay seatmate why I had said such a thing.

"Oh you know, I mean back home it's a much bigger sin." I stretched out the word, "much." I tried to de-emphasize the word, "sin." It almost sounded reasonable to me.

I realized that I might have some residual Identity Issues lying around from that whole Coming Out Thing. I decided I might have some need to actually call the number on the referral I'd been carrying around. I felt my body shaking for three hours after making the initial therapy appointment. I'd kept these Identity Issues nicely tucked away. They were doing just fine until my mother sent a rosary for Christmas and I found myself calling homosexuality a sin.

I talked to The Girl every morning and every evening. We talked a lot about Boston and New York.

"It makes more sense to live in Boston. You've got the house and the better job and I can't even get to a grocery store from where I am. Plus, I hate my job and I don't think we could fit ourselves, three cats and the dog in a Brooklyn apartment."

It sounded reasonable, but I wasn't ready. I decided only that in six months I would decide once and for all whether or not to move. I planned to stay with The Girl for a week the coming spring and do a little research on living arrangements.

"I just don't want to mess up my career. I've finally got a good thing going and I don't want to go back to being a receptionist. I've got business cards and they're on good paper stock. I want to be here a year before I move. And that's up in October."

I felt on the verge of tears all the time. I was vulnerable without The Girl in Brooklyn. The Girl pulled down my walls and then went back to her home in Boston.

I was having a hard time focusing at work. The thing was, I really didn't care about global reinsurance any more. I'd wake up in the morning with a feeling of absolute dread thinking that the world looked dark and pointless. I could force it to perk up considerably after a few cups of coffee and I'd usually manage to find a point to the day while on the express bus to work. I wanted very much to be able to wake up with all my issues, Identity and otherwise, nicely intact. I wanted to know what it felt like to have it all together. At work, I kept track of my emails for one day and sent the lot of them to The Girl.

Random Secretary—

Which budget codes should we use to pay for the Tiffany's Atlas and the books ordered for Head Guy? Thanks!

{SUBTEXT: I can't believe you didn't handle this yourself. How hard is it to call Tiffany's and ask for a leather Atlas for Pete's sake? Therefore I shall passive-aggressively bother you on every detail until you see the error of your ways.}

Random Head Guy —

Further to recent conversations concerning suggested changes to the U.S. intranet, we have requested that the IS department grant you viewing rights to the server's "testing area" where a draft version of the new home page is stored.

As soon as those permissions are in place, I'll email you the steps required for viewing the draft using Windows Explorer. If you have any questions or comments, please let me know.

{SUBTEXT: Just want you to know that the hold up here isn't me. It's the IS Dept. I'm working. They are not. Plus. I can use the phrase "further to our recent discussions" and I seriously doubt they could.}

Random Secretary—

No problem. Thanks!
{SUBTEXT: Good Lord. Stop emailing me.}

Head IS Guy—

Below is a copy of my email to Random Head Guy and Another Random Head Guy from earlier this morning.

{SUBTEXT: Politically, I should have cc'd you on the earlier email and didn't. This is me being polite. Do not get used to it. There is no reason you should have been cc'd, really, but a random IS guy emailed me and told me to cc you. I think he's wrong, but he annoys the daylights out of me. So I'll send this to you, and cc him just to keep his inbox full. I can be annoying in this respect. But I annoy politically and politely.}

Random IS Guy—

Attached are the files that need to be uploaded to the testing area. If you have any questions, please let me know.

{SUBTEXT: If I had access to the servers, I would never talk to you. You annoy me, little man.}

Dr. Professor—

A statement from the sponsor that he has read the submission and considers it to be worthy of competition should satisfy the "recommendation of the sponsor" requirement. You may also wish to include any additional remarks and comments on the quality of the paper and its significance that you feel would be helpful. Thanks again for all of your assistance with this event and if you have any further questions, please do not hesitate to contact me.

{SUBTEXT: We're sponsoring a competition. Someone asked a question. You would not believe the politics involved in answering this. One supervisor wanted to answer it one way. Another wanted a different version. Both of them had to go to outside people to form their opinions on this. Hence the vagueness of the entire thing. I couldn't begin to tell you what the entrant should write in his "recommendation." I was politically correct though and put the higher ranking supervisor's answer *first*. And then my direct supervisor's as an afterthought. This email hurt my head. All day.}

Random Entertainer Guy –

As per our phone conversation, this email will serve as confirmation for a booking on the Date at the Place in Random Place. The event is scheduled to begin with cocktails at 7:30 p.m. As discussed, we would like for you to provide circulating entertainment during the 7:30-8:00 p.m. cocktails, and a performance following dinner. You will be provided with a room for changes and storage. The $750 fee will be paid on the evening of the event. If you have any questions, please feel free to contact me via email or by phone.

{SUBTEXT: There's no real subtext, just some oddness. I'm booking a mentalist for the vice president's retreat. The mentalist talked to me for like an hour on the phone, and for some reason, accused our chairman of being a closet cross-dresser. He said, "the last time I met him, I just got from his aura that he really

*enjoyed wearing panties." I laughed. I do not understand how I
have these conversations with people. They just happen.}*

Random Head Guy—

Below is the confirmation email for the Feb. 5 event's
entertainment booking. Mr. Random Entertainer Guy indi-
cated that the booking rate is the same as last year — $750.
He will also need a room that will allow him to change and
store his props. Those details can be arranged once Your
Secretary has returned from vacation. If you need anything
further or have any questions, please let me know.

*{SUBTEXT: This is me getting all the glory and at the
same time avoiding having to do the check requisition or the
room booking. Clever, huh? I was really proud of this one.}*

Some days I did better than others. One day, I lost my earmuffs.
Somewhere within the World Trade Center – specifically on my company's floor in World Trade #2 – was a pair of pink fuzzy earmuffs. It
was throwing off my whole day. I would walk the hallways almost
whistling for them under my breath. I wanted to put up signs like
people do for lost dogs. Scrawl out a message in crayon:

*Lost: Pink Cotton Candy Earmuffs. If you find them, put them
in my cubicle. Please. Their mamma misses them.*

I made my way home that night, minus the very pink, very
happy earmuffs that complemented my fuzzy powder blue coat. It all
fell apart. There was a head-on collision somewhere in front of my
express bus in the Battery Tunnel. I got claustrophobic. A woman
stepped on my foot and failed to apologize. I did what I always did in
those situations. I sighed loudly. I came home to a phone call from
my Laundry Guy.

"I need the money. You owe $15.25. You come by and pay."

I respected his anger. He was very Yemen corporate and talked a lot about processes. Explained how he could better arrange for payment.

"You get off bus, and come by to pay it all. Next time, you leave an envelope with money in the laundry bag."

I had an urge to put his suggestions into a PowerPoint presentation and show him where he had gone awry by putting his daughter in charge of the books. I called his daughter's accounting practices into question.

"I paid the money already. Ask your daughter."

He reiterated that I still owed him money.

"I need the money. You owe $15.25. You come by and pay."

I thought he was wrong, but he was holding my clean undies hostage and I was quickly running out of negotiating power.

"Ok. I'll come by and pay. You make sure she writes it down this time."

They managed to reach an agreement and he asked me for the second time if I wanted to marry his brother.

"I throw in a goat. Just for you. You a good girl."

He laughed when he realized I thought he was joking. I was still trying to assert my identity wherever I could. But I also was trying to stay in his good graces.

"I'm off guys. I'm done with goats. Do you have any earmuffs down there?"

He didn't laugh. He hung up. I called my dad. It was his birthday. He was 54.

"Percentagewise, I'm not much older than you," he said.

"You're old enough to be my father," I shot back. We both laughed.

When we were little, my dad would take my sister and me outside to run around real quick in that space of time right before a summer thunderstorm blew up. He would take me on top of buildings where he was working on air conditioners and let me roller skate on rooftops. We played with dry ice he brought home from refrigerated trucks.

I always felt safe when he was around. He could make the world comfortable. He drove a purple truck and listened to Gene Autry. In addition to air conditioners, he fixed freezers and heaters and he loved it. Plus, he was good at it. My dad calls women "ma'am" and men "sir." I have never heard him yell. He used to play Nintendo an awful lot and he still watches movies. My dad makes excellent hush puppies.

My daddy and I used to go hunting. We'd dress in green and black and get up early. We'd get in the truck and drive to Land Between the Lakes. We'd carry our guns down trails and along streams. We would pick up a hell of a lot of nuts. Neither of us knew what kind they were. But they had a hard, green shell around them. And they were a bear to crack. We'd come home with these piles of nuts and Daddy would pour them in the driveway. Every night when he'd get home from work, the wheels of his truck would crunch a few open. He'd bend down to the gravel, pick up a nut and eat it. My dad never went to college, but he explained every instance of symbolism found in the book *Catch 22* to me. He took me inside Kentucky Dam so I could see the generators. He taught me how to fish. He taught me how to fix things. He taught me that living means you get up every morning, go to work, and when you come back home you can eat a couple of nuts out of your own driveway. I wanted to live as close into my life as he did his. I wanted to be so rooted into my world, feel so much of my own reality, that a few nuts in my driveway would be enough to make me smile.

 chapter

19

SCARED WITLESS, I stood on my therapist's corner at 103rd Street and Broadway and wondered what I was walking into. I tried to remember the last time I was so far uptown. The New York of the Upper West Side seemed far different from the New York of downtown or of Brooklyn.

I ended up liking the therapist. She made me feel normal. She made it seem okay for a girl in a sweater set to be gay and divorced and Southern and a New Yorker. She said I was remarkable and focused and I wanted to believe her. I told the therapist I took a lot of walks and always took my full lunch hour. The therapist nodded.

In an effort to subvert my company's dress code, I took to painting my fingernails rather non-corporate shades. I particularly enjoyed doing this in bars. The next day it would serve to remind me that I had a life outside of the cube.

"Listen. Just because a girl finds herself handcuffed to her own bed. Which is more difficult than you think when you don't have a headboard. We had to get on the floor and use the bed legs instead and there were people in the other room, but they left to go to MOMA so really it was fine. None of that makes me a deviant, my friend. Plus, she just has the cutest house. She built the picket fence herself. Deviants don't have picket fences."

Painting my nails, talking about handcuffs, deviants and white picket fences in Boston while sipping gin and tonics. I started telling Rachel about this email list that I ended up on which sent out several messages a day that went into great detail about how sucky it was to be gay and/or lesbian and/or deviant in general. It wasn't really the intention of the mailing list to tell people how sucky it was to be any of those things. It was supposed to be a round-up of hate crimes.

"But let me tell you honey. This weekend didn't suck, the handcuffs sure didn't suck and that blue is a great fucking color on your nails."

Despite my earlier, rather solid plan to stick it out eight more months, until October, the job was just going poorly. I sobbed every morning as soon as I opened my eyes. I would put my hand under my pillow and find a love note from The Girl. My neck hurt, my jaw was clenched and I couldn't stop crying. I was avoiding paying my bills. I ate my sausage biscuit every morning at the Burger King where I could watch commuters snaking out of the World Trade Center and off to whatever buildings they sat in until 5 p.m. I wanted life to be easy.

I thought about Boston a hell of a lot. When we were little, my mom, my sister and I were infatuated with the candy Boston Baked Beans. We loved these things and they were such a treat. You couldn't find them everywhere, so when we did find them at out-of-the-way gas stations and truck stops — usually in the middle of Illinois while we were on the way to Grandma's — we'd buy tons of them. Boston Baked Beans were such a treat.

I missed that girl.

I wondered how I could get my heart to open like that again. I wondered if I could get it to always feel the way it did when I was with The Girl. The way my mouth felt in hers, the way my hand reached for her grasp. I wanted to make her laugh, feel her sighs, her moans. Hear her whispers as they traveled down the length of my soul, through the core of my skin and into the heat of a flush on the back of my neck.

There were fantasies of a future with only her in them. I daydreamed of summer barbeques. I'd wear sneakers and sundresses or bare feet. I'd make deviled eggs and ice down the beer. Pick out the music. I'd move around the groups of people to make sure everyone felt welcome. She'd help me cook and roast ears of corn. I wondered if her dog would listen to my commands or if I'd still feel that I wasn't fully allowed to give her orders, and I'd have to wait for The Girl's dog voice to float across the lawn.

I considered what I'd set by the bedside table. How I'd introduce her to my parents. What my sister might think and how she'd like the guest room when she came to visit us. I had imaginary discussions about whether she would insist on a real tree at Christmas or if I could persuade her to think fake and possibly pink.

I tried to convince myself that I could live without her, that my future was fine, my reality was set and I was okay with her in Boston and me in New York. I thought that I would live in New York forever and ever and that two months into a relationship was far too soon to be thinking such forever-more kinds of thoughts.

But everything was taking a backseat to The Girl. The winter weather, the boring job, the need to do anything remotely constructive. I had built castles in the air and was trying to fill in the foundation. I had thought that love was for other people. I thought I knew what I wanted and it came in the shape of a corner office with a Lexus and a Prada bag. Falling in love with The Girl made me want to cry from relief.

I was fed up with the hour commute, and having to walk a mile to the grocery. I was tired of paying off the credit cards my ex-husband had run up and that I had used to escape to Brooklyn. I was caught in a financial hole and I had no idea how to get out. During one of his visits, my friend Kevin offered to help me carry my bags home from the grocery store. I refused to let him. I tried carrying them all home. Kevin looked at me making my way down Kings Highway and said,

"Just because I help you carry the bags, it doesn't make you less strong."

I thought about it a lot, but I didn't buy it. I was still trying to prove how strong I was. How independent I could be. Strong, smart, clever, lovable. I had to prove it to myself or it wouldn't be true.

I was trying to keep everything logical in making a decision about whether to move to Boston. I told myself I wouldn't do it without a job. I wanted a good job. I wanted a way to keep hold of myself. I wanted money to do that with. I was trying to achieve happiness. I was attempting to shape my reality and I had no idea what I wanted that reality to look like. So I clung to what had saved me before – a job.

It was February and I was marking my fifth anniversary in the city. A lot had changed in the years since I had moved there with my husband. I had cried when he told me we were moving. His company had him train in Birmingham before they relocated us to New York. We lived out of hotel rooms and ate takeout food the entire time. We had to turn in reimbursement forms for all of it. In Birmingham, I worked as a temp to escape the tedium. I don't remember whether I was happy or not. I must have thought that I was on my way to happy. I remember looking for cheap houses and mortgages. We lived in an apartment complex near Andrew Jackson's home. My office was next to our apartment and I would go home on my lunch hour. It was different from what I was used to, but not so bad.

Once the company moved us to New York, we had two weeks to find an apartment. I had no idea how people did things like find apartments in New York. I knew only that I should find a place in

Manhattan because figuring out anything beyond its boundaries in New Jersey or one of the other boroughs seemed too much for me. I had saved money in Nashville by selling our cars and I thought we were set for deposits. I hadn't factored in broker's fees, first month's, last month's and security.

The broker kept asking me to get a co-signer on the lease. Someone with a six-figure salary. There was no one. Instead, I started crying in her office. I used their phone to call home and cry into my mother's ear. They waived the necessity of my getting a co-signer. To get the cash they required I took out cash advances on my credit card.

My husband told me it was my responsibility to do all of this. He told me he was working and he was the one with the job, so I had to find a place to live and a way to pay for it. I went to seven different apartment buildings before I found one that was in our price range and that our couch would fit in. I was the one to go to bank after bank and have them tell me that only my own bank or a Sears store could give me a cash advance on my Discover card. I called directory services and found the nearest Sears store. I called the Sears store and asked how I could get to them by public transportation. I called the PATH information line and asked how their system worked. There was a $500 a day limit for cash advances. I went to Jersey City for three consecutive days until I had enough cash to satisfy the broker.

My husband hadn't helped with any of it.

It was three months after moving to New York before I could eat solid foods. It was six months after moving before I stopped crying myself to sleep. It hadn't been until I got the job at Mega. The job that paid me enough that I knew I could live on my own. It had taken me years after I moved to New York before I began to fall in love with the city.

I had scrapped and struggled and taken out cash advances against my future, but I had made it my own. Now I was considering a move to Boston. I didn't know if I could pull it off.

The landlady announced she was raising my rent by $100. I walked downstairs and imagined my world coming to an end. I pictured a lifetime of cereal for dinner and taking my lunch to work. Wearing cheap clothes and taking hand-outs forever and ever amen. I wondered if I would ever be able to get ahead. Get past my debts. Be able to buy a new shirt without second-guessing myself for weeks. I wanted to get over the financial sting of having charged shiny objects for the ex-husband so he would be too distracted to yell at me.

Going back and forth between Boston and New York every other weekend was crushing my heart. Every other Friday I sat on a bus. The bus that left from the Port Authority on or about 5:30 p.m. I tried to will the bus past the Triborough Bridge traffic and onto the Bruckner Expressway. Up into and through the tolls to the New York Thruway. I had a driver once try to navigate midtown rush-hour traffic by going up Fifth Avenue. It added an hour onto our time. I knew it would happen before it even did and I tried to scream at him with my mouth closed. I tried to explain to him, from my third-row seat, the importance of going up the west side and cutting through Central Park to gain access to the Bruckner. He wouldn't listen. He incurred my wrath the entire time. He never knew it.

I would spend the entire four-to eight-hour trip inside my head. I flipped around relentlessly among the pre-set radio stations on my Walkman. Ricky Martin gave way to Ludicrous and 3LW. I wouldn't stand for commercials. I wouldn't listen to the patter of DJs who were going nowhere on a Friday evening. I waited until the bus drove into Connecticut to find the country stations. There was a spot just beside the Amtrak station in Stamford, Connecticut, where only one station would come in. It took over all the frequencies and I couldn't find a way to get around the incessant Bon Jovi. Frequently the bus came to a grinding halt in traffic fleeing the city. I resigned myself to my fate. I wondered if I should read a magazine. I calculated how long it would be until I had to go to the bathroom. I told myself to be more Buddhist. To be in the moment. If I was on a bus trip to Boston, then I should be on a bus trip to Boston. I told myself I shouldn't will the future because it hadn't happened. I told myself I shouldn't live in the past because there was nothing I could do about it.

I avoided becoming obsessed with the question of "How long will this ride last?" by never looking at a map of the route from New York to Boston. The road signs meant nothing to me and I looked at them anyway. I did not want to memorize the route. I made the mistake once of asking someone what she considered to be the more-than-halfway point. Afterward, I found myself looking forward to Hartford. I wondered why I didn't just live there. After all, it was the Insurance Capital of the world. I tried to last until Hartford before having to go to the bathroom.

I was never able to sleep on the bus. I counted sheep, road signs and the bad habits of my fellow passengers. Nothing worked. I told myself stories that went nowhere. I backtracked over every second of my afternoon to see if I could have done anything differently to have saved time. Buses to Boston from New York left every half-hour. I always seemed to get on the 5:30 one. I wanted to know if it was possible to reach the Port Authority from the World Trade Center in time to go down the escalator and stand in front of Gate 62 to catch the 5 p.m. to Boston. I didn't think it was. I wondered why I had to sit in my cubicle until 5 p.m. every day. I berated myself for not being a person who could comfortably leave work at 4:30 p.m. every other Friday. I made mental notes to discuss this with my therapist. I knew I never would. I contemplated developing a section in my Palm Pilot for *Things To Discuss With My Therapist.*

I wanted to know why the woman next to me didn't put her three bags into the overhead bin rather than at her feet. I wanted to tell her that she was saving no one any time by being able to immediately grab her bags and she was crowding my feet.

I waited. I sat and waited until the bus went through the tolls and onto the Massachusetts Turnpike. Despite my better judgment I knew I was almost there. I waited for the business districts to edge closer together and the lights of a city to twinkle off the driver's windshield. I pulled out my bag and reapplied lipstick to give myself something to do. I put my Walkman on the Boston stations. We glided through the tunnels and around the construction of the Big Dig. We edged up the ramp and slowly through Boston's South Station. The driver advised us to stay in our seats until the bus had come to a complete halt. I put away my Walkman, my lipstick and my fantasies. I drifted out of my head and relaxed into myself. I looked through the windows as the bus came into the station.

And I would see her standing there. Smiling at the bus. Waiting for me at South Station. Every other Friday night.

I would take the 2:30 p.m. bus back on Sundays and would arrive at the Port Authority anywhere from 6:30 to 9 p.m. It was another hour on the subway to reach my apartment in Brooklyn. After one of the Sunday trips, I stood on a Brooklyn street corner at Kings Highway and Nostrand in the rain. I had made it home in the dark and discovered that my phone was out of service. I broke down and wandered outside to the corner.

I stood at a pay phone outside my bodega. I let a man coming from a *bar mitzvah* use the phone first. I told him I was going to be awhile. He called home. He told his wife he was on his way. He hung up and thanked me.

"No problem."

I punched in my access code and turned up my collar. I called The Girl and cried into the phone. I was trying to find a bit of comfort. Trying to find a place to rest my head in the rain, in the cold, in the dark. I watched people crossing the street. Buses passed. Men in black suits and prayer shawls streamed out of the building where the *bar mitzvah* was being held. I cried. Lost my words. Sobbed into the phone. Tried to will her the distance from Boston to New York to hold me. To make it all right.

The world was too hard. I was tired. I was tired of buses and trains and distance. I was tired of coming home to find my cat without food, I'd forgotten to tape my television shows and my phone was dead. All I had wanted to do was get back into my apartment.

The Girl and I had gotten snippy with one another at the South Station in Boston. The seat I sat in had no light. I couldn't read the *Vanity Fair* The Girl bought for my ride. I could only absent-mindedly punch the radio stations into my Walkman and let the miles pass by.

I dwelled on the way The Girl and I parted. I spent an insane amount of time going over each detail of our incredible dinner on Saturday. I had it all in my head. How I would share this with her when I got home and could call her. And the phone had been dead.

I had run out of things that interested me at work. I was sending out resumes to Boston that listed The Girl's address as my own. I wondered if I was using work-related boredom to speed up the relationship. I never thought that my craving for her might be causing me to stop caring about reinsurance.

I felt angst-ridden and exposed and vulnerable. I didn't like it much. I started planning my birthday party in my head. It was six months away, but I was seeing tiki torches and beer on ice. I wanted to dance with The Girl in a little summer dress and run barefoot in the grass. I wanted to look in her eyes and feel her arms around my waist. I wanted the grass to grow under my feet and to live within all that love.

THE FIRST time I heard from the ex, two years had passed. Two years and he sent me an email. He was accusing me of not forwarding his mail to him in an act of sabotage designed to mess up his taxes. I hadn't been in his life in two years and he was still blaming me.

He was able to find me.

I felt like crying, like hiding, like curling up into a wall someplace and never coming out. I felt like he'd come bursting into my house. Trampled on my everything.

When I told my father about the ex's email, he offered to send me a gun. He wanted to send me a Beretta.

"That's a lady's gun."

My mother had never really understood how to handle the divorce. She wanted to help, but I didn't want to give her the details. I steered conversations away from anything that might have revealed too much. We stuck to the weather and the antics of my cousins. She never asked me what happened and I never told her. She thought it was her fault somehow. I wanted it to be someone else's fault, so I let her believe that she could have stopped it.

My dad, on the other hand, made a great show. He talked constantly about wanting to come to New York and "handle things." He mentioned how effective ice picks could be. Together, we came to the conclusion that getting a restraining order would be a pretty fine idea. The full backing of New York's Finest and all that. The fact that the ex got into a rage over money and thought of blaming me. Contacted me and raged at me. After two years. It was unnerving.

It bothered me to know how much I wanted that Beretta.

I went to sleep imagining how it would be to see him die. What that gun would feel like in my hands. It was easy to judge those people on the news. Easy to hold up images of right and wrong, good and bad, evil and just.

I remembered being married and crawling down the stairs of our Manhattan apartment because I had thrown my back out and he refused to walk across the street and get me a hot water bottle. He had pulled out a chunk of my hair. He watched me throw up my dinner and screamed at me until I finished the laundry.

I remembered sitting in a closet. Banging my head against a wall over and over while he screamed at me. I could feel the fine line. That fine line between sanity and insanity. How very easy it would be to slip over it. How dark and soft and quiet that world would be. If I just let go.

I told my dad he should keep his Beretta.

I was still trying to come to terms with who I was. All the parts of me. For months after leaving my marriage, I methodically explored all the parts of my personality to find out who I really was. I went a week without make-up to determine whether or not I was a person who wore make-up. I missed my eyeliner, so I went back. I stopped balancing my checkbook to see if I really had know to the penny how much money I had. I realized I didn't care if I agreed with the bank or not about what my balance was. I discovered that I hated to cook, didn't have an interior designer bone in my body and that by leaving my marriage and coming out as a lesbian, I hadn't become someone else at all. I realized that I was, in fact, still me.

I also realized that I was one of those annoying, patronizing, liberal Christian white women. If I had a little more gumption, I would have been working in a soup kitchen. As it was, I just made a lot of assumptions about everyone lesser than me. My first assumption was that there were large numbers of people lesser than me. I traded on my whiteness. I was born of a certain class and went to college. I banked on that to get me what I wanted. I assumed without even thinking that it made me more. I had grown to be a very tolerant person and I made myself feel very moral and good and right because of that.

I picked up a book filled with essays by African-Americans — Zora Neale Hurston, Audre Lorde and Marita Bonner. I had picked it up during Black History Month because I was that patronizing. I was shocked to come upon a picture of Eldridge Cleaver speaking with great passion. He looked angry. I thought he might be about to raise his fist. It had scared me. I had grown used to seeing photos of Malcolm X. Spike Lee had done that much for me at least. But photos of angry black men with fists raised still scared me.

I knew. I knew that it would take some work to overcome the lessons I learned as the racist daughter of a racist South. I was one in a long line of poor cracker women taught to fear the black man in order to keep the social order intact.

On one of the bus rides from Boston to New York, I found myself bending over backward to prove to the two black men sitting in front of me that I wasn't racist. I told them they could lean their seats back if they wanted. Not wanting to infringe upon the Korean couple sitting behind me, I left my seat upright. I was my little white self, not wanting to "burden" the people of color sitting around me, and I left myself about two inches of seat space.

I boxed myself in with my patronizing attitude about the world. I hadn't been comfortable enough with my whiteness to take full advantage of the seat space allotted to me by the fine people of Greyhound.

It started snowing and I had a minor meltdown. My home computer didn't work, one of my cousins left a voicemail saying she wanted to discuss my homosexuality, I got a call from my sister about a boy who told her he loved her, and had a rather long and angst-ridden exchange with Rachel about my move to Boston. I felt sad and upset and frustrated and scared that I was going to lose her. I think she felt the same, so we made plans to meet and discuss everything in person.

I thought about being gay a lot. I surrounded myself with more gay magazines than most people did. I assumed it was part of the continuous coming-out process. I thought it might be a product of my being surrounded by mostly straight people during my days. When I was married, I would slip out to Chelsea to walk around. There were gay men everywhere in Chelsea. I had gone to New York Pride parades while I was married and before I ever thought about being gay myself. I would tell my husband that I was going to church. I had chosen a church in Chelsea because I liked the dramatic way they celebrated the Epiphany. On the way to the 1998 Pride, I ran into two gay men. They stopped me on the street. They were dressed in angel outfits with halos and white wings. They looked beautiful. They asked me where Sixth Avenue was and I told them. They ran off and yelled back to me,

"Happy Pride honey!"

I thought about those boys a lot. I thought of Mary being visited by angels. Given her message from God.

I would whisper to myself a million times a day,

"Love me love me love me love me love."

I wondered if I was okay, if I looked okay, if I acted okay, if I knew where my lipstick was.

There was a high school girl who got on the express bus with me. She would get off at my stop, too. Her mom would drop her off every morning. They would sit in their little hatchback until they saw the bus coming and then the girl would get out. I don't think she ever said goodbye to her mom. I think she would just get out.

There was a protocol to waiting in line for the express bus. First come, first in line. Sometimes it was confusing, but the rules were strictly enforced. If you got confused, someone would set you straight. I always thought the high school girl should get her place in line based on the time that her mom pulled up in the car.

But she always got on last.

I tried to let her get on in front of me. She wouldn't do it. She would shake her head and look down at the ground. She would do that shy, urban girl smile thing.

I imagined that since she was going to school outside of Brooklyn, she must be clever. That she must have plotted a bit to get into the high school of her choice. I imagined high school students in New York to be a tough bunch. Loud and obnoxious and traveling in packs.

This girl always let the "grown-ups" on the bus first.

I wondered how often the phrase, "love me love me love me love me" went through her mind.

I had an incredibly fraught conversation with The Girl. We were trying to decide once and for all whether she should move to New York or I should move to Boston. We were trying to decide whether anyone should move at all. Being apart was proving to be too much and her moving to New York was unrealistic. She had lived in Boston for 15 years and had a support system and a house that would be difficult to reproduce in New York. The kind of life that we wanted to lead would be easier to achieve in Boston. I was still looking for a job and there was none to be found.

I called Rachel to tell her that I was definitely moving. We cried a lot and screamed at each other for good measure, just to show one another how much the other meant. After much angst, phone calls, hanging up on one another and nasty emails, we decided to actually discuss what my moving to Boston would mean to our friendship. She had grown up outside of Boston and viewed it as a place to escape from. My moving there didn't make for an easy discussion, and as I was scared to leave New York, our conversation centered around ways to get me back into the city as much as possible. We sat around a bar and hammered out the finer details of what we both would agree to. I wrote it down on a bar napkin:

— I would visit for one week after the birth of each child she planned to have. She noted in the arrangement that I advised her to have no more than two.

— I would visit New York once a month. I was advised that this was in no way to ever be considered "too much" or "overwhelming." Her visits to Boston would occur on an "as needed" basis.

— I would visit her at her parents' Cape Cod house periodically and we hoped frequently.

— We would plan chick events (sans spouse for those who have a spouse who is a chick) quarterly.

Just thinking about being out of the local calling zone of my best friend was enough to make me cry so hard that it made my keyboard wet.

I WENT to Nashville to visit my parents. There were a lot of people in Nashville who wore overalls and didn't seem to notice. There were a lot of people who wore a lot of hairspray and were married to men with pickups. I bought cowboy boots and ate barbeque. I saw my sister and pestered her new boyfriend.

I called The Girl from a dressing room and my mom pulled the curtain back mid-sentence. I talked to my cousin. Her problem solving theory is,

"If you don't talk about it, it never happened."

My cousins laughed and nodded. If you don't talk about it, it doesn't exist.

I can't tell you how many times I've told my therapist that.

My heart ached to be so far from everything. I love The Girl. I love my city. I love my friends. I love my parents. I love my cat. I love my sister.

I told my parents I was moving out of the city. They suggested Nashville. My dad offered me his truck.

It was hard not to feel I'd let them down.

My plane from Nashville landed at LaGuardia a full hour early. I had my luggage ten minutes after landing. I got a cab right away. The cab driver knew an honest-to-God shortcut to my house in far, far Brooklyn that saved us twenty minutes of travel time and reduced my fare by $7.

I got out of the cab wearing my new cowboy boots. I stood in the median that ran the length of Kings Highway. I set down my bags, stretched out my arms and said,

"Hi Brooklyn. I'm home."

Rachel decided we needed a night out with some friends. I tousled my hair. I put on a red halter top with "Cowgirl" spelled out in gold lettering. I found some tight jeans and put on my cowboy boots. They made me feel like stomping.

The club was in a lower midtown neighborhood I had worked in at one time. You had to walk down dark stairs to reach it. Rachel had gone to high school with the woman who worked the door. When she wasn't working the door, she worked as a dominatrix. The dominatrix sat on a barstool and stamped our hands. I ordered a Jack and Coke. I was trying to get up the nerve to be in this place.

The bar started filling up with people. We had gotten there at midnight and it was almost 2 a.m. before things started moving. I was on my third Jack and Coke and I watched a guy dressed in lipstick and eye shadow take a riding crop to his date, who was galloping like a horse. I walked upstairs and watched women clad in bits of leather dancing under black lights. One of the girls we were with wanted to make out with a guy in the corner. He kept trying to kiss me. I kissed him back and moved his mouth so that it was on hers instead. He never noticed. An Asian woman came up and asked me what I was drinking. She left and came back with a Jack and Coke. She put her arm on my bare shoulder and told me I looked hot. She started kissing my ear and whispered,

"I've always wanted to be with a woman."

Her husband walked up and asked what was going on.

"I think she was looking for you," I said.

He put his hand on my ass and said, "No, it looks like she was looking for you."

I placed his hand on his wife's arm and walked away.

I found Rachel and started talking. I was on my fifth drink. I felt a hand on my breast, groping me. It moved down to my crotch and I didn't move. I was drunk and it felt good. I turned around to see who the hand belonged to. It was a friend of Rachel's so I let the hand stay. I took another drink and leaned backwards. Rachel raised an eyebrow and tried to talk to someone else. I forgot where I was and that I was in love. I was drunk and it was dark and the place seemed on the verge of a really good evil.

At 3 a.m., Rachel pulled my arm and told me we were leaving. I had gone too far. She got us a cab back to her place where I slept it off. The next morning, I took another cab home. I walked into my apartment and threw up.

I found someone's lipstick on my arm. I took a hot shower and tried to wash out the memory of the club. I dried off and called The Girl.

I told her I no longer had any doubts. I wanted to move.

I walked around the apartment in a daze for the rest of the weekend. I felt lost. Stepping outside of my boundaries, going past my morals, had shaken me.

I missed The Girl. She grounded me and made me feel powerful. She kept me from spinning out of control and I missed her badly. Without her, I lost it. I sat in my pajamas all day eating ice cream. I downloaded porn and looked for erotica, trying to find her. Trying to fill myself up.

I loved The Girl and I wanted a life with her and only her. New York and my desire to experience all that I thought I had missed out on had loosened its hold on me during that night in the club's dark basement.

I would sometimes take the train to Boston instead of the bus. It cost more, but was infinitely more comfortable. They had renovated Penn Station during the time I lived in New York. They added an electronic big board to announce the arrivals and departures and no longer used the one that clicked and clacked its way down. There was a new, large sitting area for Amtrak customers only. Everything was in neon and the place still smelled. Penn Station smelled worse than the Port Authority. I gagged every time I went there. The bathrooms reeked so much that my eyes watered and I looked around for the nearest trash can in which to hurl.

I asked for Good Friday off and took the train to Boston for Easter. I had time to kill, so I sat down at one of the food courts to eat a slice of pizza. A homeless woman sat down next to me and the stench from her tray was unbelievable. She had piled it high with tomatoes and lettuce and onions from the free condiment bar that was in the middle of the food court.

She eyed the books I had just bought.

"Those your school books?"

"Yeah." Taking the train was making me feel polite and gracious.

"What're you studying?"

"Economics." I nearly made myself laugh.

"That's a harsh subject!"

"No kidding." I was getting into it and so was she.

"I'm studying technology."

"Now that's a harsh subject," I said.

"No kidding. Where do you go to school?"

Before I could even think, I blurted out, "Kingsborough Community."

I couldn't believe it. I was sitting there having a fake conversation with a homeless woman and I couldn't even get myself to consider NYU, Columbia or Harvard. Instead I portrayed myself as a second-year economics student at Kingsborough Community College. The homeless woman walked away and I didn't blame her.

The phone in my apartment went down again, and I arranged for service from the office. I loved that what had passed for installation of service in my apartment was basically running a phone line off of my landlords' phone, down the outside of the house, along the ground, and into my house. It was no surprise to me that whenever it rained, my phone would go out.

The phone company told me they would arrive in the service window of 8 a.m. to 7 p.m. I told them I considered that more along the lines of a "day" rather than a "window."

I realized that if at 8:27 a.m. I'm drinking coffee in a Manhattan Burger King, I'm nowhere near my Brooklyn apartment. Rather than take a day off work for the phone company's "window," I attached a long phone line to the old rotary phone I owned. I ran the cord out the front door and left a little note for the phone guy explaining that this should be considered his "access to my indoor line."

He called me to tell me I was very creative.

I told him if he had such a creative definition of "service window" then I would have a creative definition of "allowing access to the inside phone line."

He laughed and said my phone was fixed.

Being away from The Girl during the week was difficult. I lived for Fridays and cried when we parted every Sunday. The worst, though, was when life interfered and we weren't able to see one another on the weekend. I was never good about it when The Girl chose not to travel the four hours to Brooklyn. I tried hard not to be bitchy and desperate. I told myself that if she needed a Saturday to herself, she could have it. I swore that I wasn't going to pick up the phone and talk to her for the entire 48 hours.

I attempted, through passive aggressive conversations, to tell her that she should be in Brooklyn helping me clean out my closets and get ready to move to Boston. When she didn't hear my non-verbal phone cues. I couldn't stop thinking,

"She doesn't love me, she doesn't love me, she doesn't love me."

She called me at work and asked if there was something I wasn't telling her. I started crying in the cubicle and told her to hold on. I grabbed my cell phone and took the elevators downstairs. I walked outside and stood in the middle of the plaza in front of the fountain. I thought running water would cover up my crying. She asked me if I needed her to come to Brooklyn that weekend.

"I can't tell you that. Come if you want to come."

She wouldn't take it as an answer.

"I need you to tell me if you want me to come to Brooklyn."

I cried harder. No one had ever wanted to know my opinion. No one ever had asked if they could do something for me. I didn't know how to answer. I started to shake. She was asking me to tell her that I needed her. That I needed to hold her. That I needed to hear her voice. That I needed her to be with me.

I had given up wiping off my tears. A group of schoolchildren walked past me in twos. They were holding hands with one another. Using the time-tested buddy method of navigating the unknown. They turned their heads to see me sobbing.

I held the phone away from the fountain and said,

"Please. Please come to Brooklyn. I need you here. I can't go without seeing you."

She hung up the phone and started driving. I went into the mall under the towers and found a make-up counter. I fixed my eye shadow and put on more face powder. I tried to get my hands to stop shaking before I took the elevator back to my cubicle. I sent out more resumes to companies in Boston.

We had spent a beautiful weekend together in Boston. We drove past the skyline and the Charles River and there were white city lights and skyscrapers and she used the city to wrap her love for me around.

She whispered,

"That's where I'd take you to ask you to marry me."

She took my hand in hers and kissed it. I kept falling in love.

We had walked to the Commons and watched the Swan Boats and the ducks and the green, green grass. I had neglected to wear socks and developed blisters. She switched shoes with me. She kept capturing my heart.

Instead of staying with her in Boston, I had forced myself to go back to Manhattan and head out to New Jersey for the senior leaders' retreat. I was convinced that they had insisted I attend purely to make sure the PowerPoint presentations worked and the karaoke guy showed up. I questioned the wisdom of setting up a karaoke night for a hundred underwriters and actuaries, but my boss insisted.

I took the train from Boston back to New York and had a car service meet me at Penn Station. It took us an hour to drive from Manhattan to the off-site location where the retreat was being held. I grew more and more pissed off as the driver put miles between me and Manhattan. I didn't want to be at the event. I didn't want to be away from my apartment in Brooklyn and I didn't want to be away from The Girl in Boston.

I was pissed off that they were treating me so casually. That they didn't care about my Brooklyn apartment. That they thought I was interested in actuaries singing karaoke.

Throughout the two-day event, I missed The Girl in a kind of dramatic fashion that had me calling her on my cell phone during breaks in the meetings. I sneaked online whenever possible to see if any jobs from Boston had come through. I almost didn't care whether I had a job waiting for me. Drifting from place to place as a temp seemed much more interesting than being treated like someone who could only be responsible for PowerPoint presentations. The prospect of going without medical insurance, though, scared the hell out of me and I continued to hold out hope for a job offer.

It turned out that my boss had been right about karaoke night – it was a blast. I discovered one of the underwriters had grown up near my hometown. Our accents matched and we put them to good use singing every Willie Nelson title there was. We made a stunning duet.

Afterward, the head of the San Francisco office and I went out for drinks. We decided that 10 p.m. in Jersey meant that it was cocktail hour somewhere. And we came to the conclusion that conventions, off-site meetings and all after-5 work-related activity should be banned.

The rest of the week seemed like drudgery. It was all I could do to get to a weekend. I was connected to The Girl primarily through our emails.

Click refresh. Click refresh. Come into my world. Please.

I needed a quick dose of reality. I needed to call my mother and arrange for my father's upcoming sightseeing trip to New York. I needed to send my sister's birthday present and buy a Mother's Day card. I needed to pay my American Express, my Sprint, my cell phone and my Visa. I mailed one bill and felt exhausted. I called to check my balance and felt overwhelmed. I did a phone interview and vowed that I had hit the limit.

I held myself to impossibly high standards that nevertheless felt far too low. I hadn't swept my floors in weeks and the litter needed changing. There were boxes to drag outside. Piles of papers to do something with.

Click refresh. Click refresh. Come into my world. Please.

We spent Sunday in Boston with friends and I remembered snippets of the conversation. Looks and hugs and pats. Someone uttered the phrase, "leather pants." I kept remembering that. Leather pants. I wanted to be in Boston. I had more reasons to be in New York.

Click refresh. Click refresh.

There were mornings when I felt young and cute and well-dressed. I would play it up for whoever I thought might be watching. I would sling my black bag over my shoulder and flip through my

Walkman as if I were more hip than anyone else on the express bus could ever be. I would pull out my Palm Pilot and read the *Wall Street Journal*. I pretended that I had stocks, cared about the weather in Miami or had a flight into O'Hare that needed my attention.

I needed to remind myself that I was young. I used to beat myself up for having gotten married at such an early age. I used to call myself stupid. *How could you have done that? What were you thinking? Who the hell were you?*

The truth is, I was a person who needed to get married. I needed to have society's approval to feel valid. I needed to have the ring on my finger to know I was loved. I needed to get the hell out of Kentucky and I knew that he would get me out of the South. That marriage gave me all those things.

When I no longer needed those things, I no longer needed the marriage.

Now, I needed to be in Boston.

I was doing well in the world, and I started to poke at things to stir up a little extra drama in my life. I would sometimes call my old phone number to see if my ex-husband was still living in our old apartment. I wanted to be told that he had gotten fired from his job and was living on the streets. Usually I would get the answering machine and know that he was still living in Manhattan and not in his parents' basement. One day, I called from work and he answered the phone.

I hung up, but my phone rang immediately telling me he had gotten the number off caller ID. I let it go into voicemail, and when I checked my messages, I heard him breathing. I called Roxanne to get her read on the situation and she told me,

"If neon were free and abundant, you would have a flashing *Al-Anon* sign over your head."

Roxanne had a theory that adult children of alcoholics stirred up drama to recreate the drama that surrounded our home lives as children. That was a neat theory and maybe it was true, but things were never dramatic in my childhood home. The scenario around my dad's drinking was that we were all in tune with his needs, to the extent that ours never mattered. It made us all unaware of our own boundaries, where we left off and others began. It was always about second-guessing the alcoholic's motives and needs. Which is why I thought I stirred up the drama by calling the ex-husband. I wanted to see where he was, what he was up to, in case I needed to be aware of it later.

Every other week, before my therapy appointment, I would do an examination of conscience similar to what I had done before going to confession as a kid. The topic that came up most often was my dad's drinking. The last time he had visited me, he had drunk an entire bottle of Maker's Mark. In one weekend.

The therapist helped, for a while. But then she began to annoy the living hell out of me. She talked a lot and dismissed most of my concerns as perfectly normal. I decided I didn't want to pay someone to tell me I was normal. I wanted her to tell me I was special, beautiful, gorgeous in my angst and fraught with unique traits. I told her I no longer needed her services.

I dove into work in an attempt to forget the drama, and managed to write a truly stunning speech for the CEO to deliver at a reception. It was focused on the glories of actuarial science and I was proud of myself.

I showed it to my boss and she nodded her head and walked away. After the speech itself was delivered, I had two people email me and ask me for copies of it. My boss was never going to tell me I was good, but I knew better. I knew I was great.

 chapter

22

I SPOKE to The Girl while she was doing yard work. I sat on a post and talked and felt my face getting red from the sun. I talked about being in high school marching band. I had loved being in marching band. I had marched in parades at Mardi Gras and in the Fiesta Bowl. I had gone places in that band. I nearly quit every year. Being in marching band was hard and hot and sweaty. We would learn our half-time show in August. Kentucky summers were 90 degrees and 90 percent humidity. I would think it couldn't get any hotter and then it did. We marched anyway.

Once, during a break in the middle of one of those camps, I sat under a tree and complained about being hot. A boy looked at me complaining and winced. He said, "You know what? We're all hot. We're all sweaty. You're not the only one."

I thought of that statement a lot. I told The Girl about it.

I told her how we marched even when we didn't want to and when we didn't think we could go any further. I learned how to be proud in that band.

I felt like I was sitting under that tree complaining about how hard everything was and that boy was telling me,

"You know what? We're all hot. We're all sweaty. You're not the only one."

Sitting in The Girl's house, I realized that life outside the city of New York could be pleasant. There were two little neighborhood girls playing with The Girl's dog in the backyard. They kept making up commands for the dog. The dog was constantly confused but loving it. She ran around and licked everyone and the girls fell into a heap giggling.

We had dinner with The Girl's friends. The Girl had grilled salmon that was so delicious I ate slowly, shut my mouth and tried to hold onto that taste. We had been picking at each other that afternoon. The distance between Boston and New York was taking its toll.

Over dinner, one of The Girl's friends offered me a six-month temp job. She needed someone to answer phones for her department. I didn't know what to say. I wanted a Magic 8 ball that would give me all the answers, or at least the answer that I needed. I wanted to feel sure and confident about the decision either way.

I got on the bus to New York City the next day and stared out the window as Boston fell away. I thought about the temp job. There would be no benefits, no paid sick days, no paid vacation days. I would be leaving a job I had struggled for. A job with my own business cards, one that occasionally used my talents. I would be answering phones. The pay was decent, but not sufficient, and I would be dependent on The Girl for money, for shelter and even for transportation since I didn't have a car. It seemed foolish to move just for love. Foolish to uproot my reality, my friendships, my support network, my security and my career, just for the chance of love.

Everything I had gone through in my life told me I could depend only on myself. Everything I knew told me that I should never depend on anyone for anything, even if it was just a ride to work. Everything in my world taught me that it was dangerous to fall in love. It scared me to think about depending on someone else. It frightened me even though I knew it was pitiful and sad to live only for a career.

Leap of faith. That's what they called falling love. Taking a leap of faith, putting your trust into someone's hands and taking the responsibility of their trust being in yours. Love. My knees had buckled at train stations and I had awaked at 3 a.m. wondering why she wasn't next to me. Why couldn't I touch her? What was I doing in a place where I couldn't touch her?

When I got back to Brooklyn, I cried a lot. I tried to make a decision. I ran the numbers and priced U-Hauls and packing boxes. I contemplated all the pitfalls, all of them. I called my bank three times to check my balances.

I realized no one was ever going to give me anything and no one could take away all that I had done. If I had been able to forge a career in New York City, then I could do the same in Boston. I had come from a long line of very determined women and I wasn't about to question those genes. Plus, I loved The Girl.

I decided to take the temp job and move to Boston.

My right eye would twitch whenever I got anxious. I had to defrost the freezer before I vacated the apartment. There were grapes in the bottom drawer that had been there for two months and a red, sticky substance that I thought might be from Chinese takeout on the bottom shelf.

Twitch.

I sent an email to my mother informing her of the move. I figured it was the least I could do. The most I could do would be to tell her that I was moving for love, but I still wasn't up to having that conversation. She emailed me back right away and wrote, "I love you and want you to be happy!" I realized that no matter what our differences, she loved me.

Twitch.

I had to develop a reason for turning in my resignation. A reason that wouldn't send my boss on a tear for the two weeks remaining, but that was still pretty close to the truth. Usually when I resigned jobs I would say that I had gotten a better opportunity. I couldn't say that in this situation. I decided the truth would be a good idea and I would tell her that, "My partner lives in Boston and we've contemplated whether to combine our households in New York, or in Boston. We've decided Boston is the better fit for us." I just wanted to be able to use the phrase, "combine households." It made me sound rich and I liked that.

Twitch.

I kept crying when I thought too much about leaving New York. The company's computer guy told me that he thought I was, "lifelong Brooklyn." I told him I was. I told myself that my heart was in another place. I didn't want to say goodbye to the city.

People kept asking me why I had decided to move. What made me know it was the time to go. I had a pat little story that I would tell most people, about coming back to New York from Boston to a subway that smelled of urine. Of having to drag my suitcase around a subway that kept being delayed and rerouted. But that was a story about not liking New York, and the reason I was moving had nothing to do with not liking New York.

The actual tipping point had been a trip to The Girl's neighborhood liquor store for ice. I had walked there. I jaywalked through the intersection. I was honked at. A Hispanic woman hanging at the laundry on the corner eyed me. Two kids got off the sidewalk to let me pass. I got to the store and laid my dollar on the counter.

"Bag of ice," I said and turned to get it.

The counter guy, barely looking up, noticed I was wearing The Girl's Red Sox jacket and said,

"Sure thing hon."

That was it.

I wrote out all the reasons I was moving to Boston so I wouldn't forget them. My throat was sore and I wondered why I was still doing so much work when I was leaving the job. I couldn't sleep because I was making detailed plans of everything that needed to be done before I moved. I had to turn off the electric, get the mail forwarded, pack, hire a U-Haul, hire guys to load the truck, unload the truck and I had exactly two weeks to get it all done.

I made lists, checked lists and kept thinking about the first person I had ever kissed. It had been a girl, and I had kissed her behind the Frogger machine at the skating rink. We had gone with her parents to pick up her older brother and found him behind the pinball machine with a girl. It looked fun to us so we got in the space behind the Frogger machine and made out. When we got back to her house, we went into her bedroom and did things that I didn't imagine girls did.

A year later her dad got transferred and she moved away. I cried so hard. My mom just held me and stroked my hair and told me "You'll find other friends." I remember saying,

"Not like her."

I outed myself to a coworker when I told him I was leaving. We talked about how stupid our jobs were. He said, "At least the pay is decent. It's boring as hell, but they pay us well. It's like golden handcuffs here."

I nodded.

He was trying to get transferred to London because he wanted to work overseas. He was hesitant to go because he didn't want to have to quarantine his cat. We looked out the window of the corporate boardroom. If you tilted your head just right, you could get a view of the Hudson River. It was late afternoon and there was an odd pink glow in the building as the sun set. I told him I was nervous about moving, about giving up my career. He looked at me and said,

"Hey, get out of here while you can."

I wrote the resignation letter. I was scared to hand it to my boss.

I told myself that if I could walk out of a marriage, I could do anything. She still scared me. She couldn't kill me, but she could make me feel small and that was the thing that scared me most.

I kept popping up over my cubicle to see if she was in her office. I looked like one of those arcade games where you're supposed to club the monster when he pops out of the hole.

When I saw her round the corner, I made my way into her office. She handled it much more gracefully than I thought she would. She asked if my resignation was due to anything that she had done.

Once suitably assured, she actually smiled. She didn't even flinch when I told her that the "partner" came with a pronoun of "she."

After we were done talking, she came by every ten minutes to ask, "What's happening with the color copies?"

It was like there was a party she was missing. Like she was inquiring about mutual friends or something. I told her, "They're printing out. Color copies take awhile."

I couldn't believe we were having this conversation.

I smiled to myself.

I had quit.

I had been the kid who never missed a day of school. I had gone through twelve years of school and missed three days. One of them I had been faking it. I never took sick days. In the seven years that I had been out of college, I had taken only two-and-a-half sick days. The half was when I put my cat to sleep. I rarely took vacations, and I had quit.

I had quit my job and the world hadn't stopped spinning.

There was a certain kind of frantically Zen state that my mind reached after having given two-weeks' notice. I was still desperate to be turning a cog, any cog and I had taken the cog away from myself. I was a hamster without a wheel.

I spent a lot of time in my head and I ran through lists of all the possible problems that would arise upon moving to Boston. I analyzed every relationship I had ever been in. I wished I had kept the bedroom window open for the cat. I composed lists of all the ways living in Boston would be fantastic and remarked upon how easily the move came together. I tried to figure out where to put my couch. How my silverware would fit into her kitchen drawers. Why I had a silver-plated ice bucket.

I alternated between over-sentimentalizing my time in New York with sappy poetics and compiling a list of ways the city was making my life miserable. I was edging close to feeling resentful of New York for taking so much energy, for making me want to be in it rather than easily moving in with The Girl. I was feeling resentful of the city because I had to live there for two more weeks instead of being in her arms.

I got overwhelmed with it all. I left work shaky and losing my ground. I went home and hid under the covers. I wanted to cry but it seemed too much trouble. I wanted to get myself excited, but it seemed too out of reach. So I hid under the covers.

I opened all the windows and the breezes got cool. I pulled the covers over my head and made it dark and silent. I shut out the birds and wouldn't let the cat find her way in with me. Every night I would pack. I was throwing things out. There seemed so much to be done and so little time. There were so many things. Notebooks, papers, pens and journals. I had three boxes of crayons and computer disks that contained no files. Books that I would never read, magazines and clothes.

Every time I saw those boxes I remembered the last time I had packed. I remembered moving out of the apartment. I hadn't had the luxury of two weeks to pack that time. That time I had to bring home all the boxes and pack and move out in less than 12 hours. This time was different. This time I had two weeks.

I found the whole process overwhelming. There was too much going on that I couldn't control. I wanted someone to hold my hand.

I wanted someone to understand. Someone to tell me that it would be okay. I wanted to know what life was going to be like in

Boston. I wanted to know that I was doing the right thing by moving.

I hid under the covers until The Girl called. She made me laugh, made me feel stable and secure again.

I missed her.

Three days left on the job, and my boss was driving me insane. She kept asking me when I had sent an article on a claims seminar to the Paris office. She got snippy with me because I didn't know the exact date. I told her I would find out. She said, "You do that and let me know because we have to keep some kind of controls on this."

I wondered why she thought I cared.

She came back two hours later, waving a copy of a brochure I had printed weeks before. She told me that one of the bosses had found a mistake in it. She told me that mistakes in brochures were why I should proof things very carefully. She told me this was very embarrassing for her.

My face got flushed after the boss walked away. I knew I had proofed the damn thing because I had gone to the trouble of buying myself a candy bar and soda to keep myself occupied while I did it. I had made it into a little proofing party because I had a hangover at the time and caffeine and sugar were necessary for staying awake.

I checked my files, which I had just moved to my recycling bin as part of cleaning out my desk. I found the galleys and blues that I signed off on and smiled. I had been right. I had proofed them correctly. The printing error had been the printer's fault, not mine. And I had proof.

I took them into the boss' office and showed her. She smiled and said, "Take those upstairs and show my supervisor that we had checked these properly. I knew you were usually so good about these things."

After lunch, I had my exit interview with the woman in Human Resources. Out the window behind her, I watched the Staten Island

Ferries moving through the harbor. She wished me well and I handed her my World Trade Center ID. I walked out of the building with a box of my personal belongings. It was a small box.

The Girl found out that her company offered domestic partnership benefits from day one that we, "declare that we're responsible for one another's welfare." She sent me the form and it was all worded in nice corporate-speak that made me grin. We were going to start living as a couple. I would get to come home and tell the woman I loved about my day. Sometimes we would go to the movies together. I had a momentary worry that living as a couple would mean I would have to change who I was. And then I remembered. I wasn't marrying my ex again.

This time I knew who I was.

I had questioned my sexuality, spirituality, what I liked to read, whether or not I wore lipstick, what I did in my spare time. I learned that I could stand — not only on my own two feet, but on my head. And I knew how to whistle. I liked to eat my eggs sunny-side up. This time, I was in love and I knew who I was.

I had wanted a certain kind of comfortable life so badly I had wished it into existence with a few half-voiced dreams and a U-Haul. *Reinvent yourself. Reinvent yourself. If you don't like the life you're leading, lead another one.* This time, it was easy to pick up and go because I knew I controlled my destiny. There were very few things in the world that I *had* to do. I didn't have to stay in Kentucky. I didn't have to stay married. I didn't have to live in New York. And I no longer had to be alone.

Rachel and I said our good-byes by going to Coney Island and riding the Cyclone. We sat on the boardwalk and ate burgers. We had long conversations. We walked around Sheepshead Bay. We went back to Park Slope for pedicures and massages. I was leaving my best friend and the city I loved. I didn't want to say good-bye to either of them.

At the end of the day, I handed Rachel a key to the house in Boston and hugged her. We both started to cry, so we had to walk away. I yelled back over my shoulder,

"See ya later."

I saw tears flowing down her face.

It was hard to stand in the middle of the empty apartment. The movers were carrying my things out the door and I had turned my keys over to my landlords. Everything was boxed up, wrapped up and put away. The Girl stood next to me, holding me and wiping away my tears. All the little pieces of the place I had made into a home were sealed with packing tape.

I had come to this place scared. I had wanted to move some place where he would never find me and this place in far, far Brooklyn had been perfect.

I had been lost. I was small and hidden and I had forgotten who I was. Most people carry around an image of battered women cowering in corners waiting to be beaten.

That image is wrong.

I wasn't the battered woman cowering in a corner, and I doubt that any of us who have been beaten stayed because we were stupid. Put up with it because we had no self-esteem. We put up with it because we had no way out. We fought back in the ways that we could. He would hit and I would grab a butcher knife and wave it in his face until he backed down. I would run out the door to escape the reach of his fists. I would come back because I had nowhere else to go.

Everyone imagined that battered women cowered in corners, but the easiest thing to do is to sit in a corner. Slip into the darkness. There had been times I edged toward that fine line of insanity. Times I had almost given in to his madness. It looked so easy. So goddamn simple. Let it slip. It'll be easier if I just stop thinking, stop feeling, stop caring.

I never slipped. I never stopped caring and I never gave up hope. And one day the world had come together by giving me a job, money, friends and the opportunity to make a home in far, far Brooklyn. I had wanted to live some place where he would never find me, and in the end I managed to find myself.